"Pesare hits it out of the park with *Back in the Game*. Great tale about the R.I. State Police that keeps you on edge of your seat. A MUST READ."

–Joe Pistone, FBI Agent, author of *Donnie Brasco: My Undercover Life in the Mafia*

"Pesare effectively captures the human experience of working for the RI State Police Intelligence Unit, specifically our organized crime investigations. It surpasses the typical police procedural, offering a detailed portrayal of the personal lives, relationships, and hardships faced by all involved in the fight against the mob."

–Col. Brendan Doherty, RI State Police (ret.), co-author of *It's Just the Way It Was: Inside the War on the New England Mob*

"*Back in the Game* is tantamount to a level 5 white water rush on the rapids of Maine. Pesare has created an astonishing inside view inside both the Rhode Island State Police and New England organized crime depicting the personal pitfalls that beset everyone affected by both entities. Pesare is what many of us in law enforcement would call 'the real deal,' avoiding the political pressures that can haunt any officer charged with the trust of the state. Bravo, Anthony!"

–Armen Garo, Shift Commander, Lt. East Providence Police Department (Ret.) and actor known for his appearances in *The Departed, The Sopranos, American Hustle,* and *The Wolf of Wall Street,* among many others

A GINO PETERSON NOVEL

BACK IN THE GAME

ANTHONY M. PESARE

To the late Capt. Donald F. Kennedy Jr. (ret.) Rhode Island
State Police, Class of 1974

*"Think where man's glory most begins and ends,
and say my glory was I had such friends."*
William Butler Yeats

PROLOGUE
Fall 1987

The drive from Rhode Island to Colchester, Vermont, is almost six-and-a-half hours. Gino Peterson traveled from his apartment in Cranston through Massachusetts and New Hampshire to his destination near Lake Champlain. Driving through rustic villages and sweeping mountain vistas did not lift Gino's spirits. Gino was on the verge of checking himself into a rehabilitation center for first responders suffering from trauma and resulting addictions. Gino had seen it all in his many years in law enforcement, but nothing could have prepared him for this. It was a brutal battle unlike any other he had ever faced. The stakes were high, and the situation was dire. Gino knew that he had to give it his all, even if it meant putting everything on the line.

Corporal Michelle Urban, also a member of the state police, was driving him. Their conversation was quiet and heavy, burdened by their tumultuous relationship. As they moved through Lebanon on Route 93, Gino glanced over: "Thanks for taking me up here."

Michelle looked at him, squinting as the midmorning sun rushed into the car. "I'm just happy you're getting the help you need."

Gino nodded and lowered his head. He was thinking of everything that had brought him to this point. "I embarrassed myself, my family, and the department. I just desperately wanted to get back into the Intelligence Unit. I wanted things to be like they were."

Michelle looked at him with crystal green eyes, the same eyes that had mesmerized him when they first met. "Gino, I know the costs of reclaiming your reputation, especially when your personal life isn't cooperating."

Gino reflected on the chain of events that had brought him to this point. First, he lost two key witnesses in a high-profile trial that he was assigned to guard. He had prepared as best as he could, and it was unfathomable to believe that a federal agent would get corrupted by the mob. When Agent Karakides, sworn to protect both witnesses as they were leaving the courthouse, shot them in broad daylight, it was devastating. Gino then suffered a demotion in the department. Did the punishment fit the crime? Probably not, but in law enforcement, that's the kind of punishment one suffers. The pound of flesh must come from somewhere.

Of course, Michelle knew all this because they were her witnesses too. Did she also know about his back injuries? The pressures of being a cop in general? That pure, good feeling we all seek?

Gino wasn't sure how to describe the feeling of well-being that Vicodin had given him, but he felt he had to try. "It was like I was floating over all my fears, stresses, and life. I needed it to get through everything else in my life. Or at least I thought I did."

"Is that why you needed Renée too?" Michelle's voice dripped with a contempt she didn't try to hide. Renée was a former prosecutor and a professor at a local community college.

"Michelle, Renée packed up and left. She told me I wouldn't commit to a life with her because I still have feelings for you. Are you happy now?"

The silence returned like a curtain coming down at the end of a play. The sun bathed Gino's face and provided a warmth that he thought might almost feed his soul.

He remembered the sense of urgency he felt as he packed his backpack to go to rehab. He carefully chose the items he needed for his stay, including photos that reminded him of the life he was fighting for. These photos had emotional significance and helped him stay positive during difficult times.

After he had finished packing, he had sat and waited for Michelle to pick him up. Now, on the ride, he took the stack of old family photos from his lap and looked at them individually. He remembered fond memories and moments he cherished with his loved ones. The photos brought him comfort and strength, reminding him of the importance of his mission.

One showed a twenty-four-year-old Gino dressed in the RI State Police uniform. He was leaning against a Harley Davidson police motorcycle, staring back at the camera lens with an easy grin of satisfaction and relief. It was 1974, and Gino had just graduated from the training academy. Tall and skinny after three months of grueling training. He recalled something his father often said, "If I only knew then what I know now."

Gino's dad was not in any of the pictures, and Gino felt he could add that to the list of reasons his efforts to self-medicate had gotten out of control. Albert Peterson had passed away in a car accident when Gino was just ten years old. The police told his mom, Teresa, that his father had driven off the road in an unfortunate event. Gino never believed it was an accident. But when a mob member who was suspected of causing the accident, Bobo Detroia, went away to prison for an unrelated homicide, Gino had tried to let it go.

At the time of his dad's passing, the family had lived in a tenement apartment in the Federal Hill section of Providence. In the seventies, the "Hill" was the hub for Italian immigrants. Atwells Ave., the neighborhood's main street, was lined with shops and food markets. He inhaled the mix of aromas from numerous restaurants. The Italian chatter and the honking created a symphony reminiscent of Leonard Bernstein's *West Side Story*.

Gino wanted to show Michelle a picture without distracting her from the road, so he flashed it briefly.

"Do you remember this?" he asked. The question was gentle despite all the sarcastic remarks both had made so far.

Sgt. Michelle Urban, Gino, and the detectives from the Intelligence Unit were posed for a group photo. Viewing the photo evoked memories of their illicit love. The aftermath of their fractured relationship was yet another reason he began taking more pills.

"Of course, I remember, Gino. Those were the good times. The times when we never believed they would hold our mistakes against us forever."

▪ ▪ ▪

Gino expected his assigned room to be like a cell. Instead, it was like a hotel room, tastefully furnished with a large bed, desk, and tiled shower. For the next three months, this would be his home. And, indeed, his room became a welcome respite from the endless group and individual counseling sessions. He thumbtacked the pictures from the Intelligence Unit, where he was transferred after five years in the Uniform Division, to a small corkboard to help him feel more comfortable. Every trooper aspired to become a detective in those days. You could be placed in the Auto Theft or the Narcotics Unit. However, the Intelligence Unit was the most prestigious of all because it investigated and prosecuted organized crime. Working on wiretaps and surveillance was fascinating, especially when it involved tracking people in mob hits.

Many factors had driven Gino to succeed within the state police. Gino's Uncle Earl was a state trooper and the family's hero. He had received commendations for arresting a bank robber who had escaped from prison, which cemented his place on a pedestal. There was also the desire to combat the image of all Italians as somehow associated with organized crime.

Gino was only half Italian, with the other half Swedish, but it bothered him that Italian cops had the reputation of being untrustworthy. Not all Italians were on the take. And then there was the death of his father. Even though Gino never knew the exact details of that night, he had never been able to shake his suspicion that the mob was somehow involved, which drove him to make and win cases against the Mafia. And now he had thrown away any chance of regaining his position because he could not control his addiction. As it turned out, he was far from alone in this facility among people who would do anything to get their old lives back.

■ ■ ■

"Group in fifteen," was the announcement after the knock on the door. Gino shuffled down the corridor wearing sweatpants, a long-sleeved URI shirt, and Nikes. At the end of the corridor was a large meeting room with twelve metal folding chairs arranged in a circle.

As soon as everyone had settled down, Dr. Pagliuca began the session. Audrey, as she liked to be called, was about fifty years old, with long, curly, and messy red hair. Her hazel eyes and high cheekbones gave her an exotic appearance. An Irish knit sweater, brown corduroy skirt, and leggings completed Audrey's comfy outfit.

She had a deep voice that demanded attention. "Hello, everyone. Good afternoon."

The temptation to respond to her was too great to ignore. "Good afternoon," everyone said in unison.

"Does anyone want to share first?"

After several minutes of silence, a young woman stood up and said, "My name is Philomena, but everyone calls me Phil, and I'm an addict." Philomena then described a life that was as dissimilar from Gino's in its external factors as could be imagined: occupation, family situation, stressors, and background. But the slippery slope by which she had convinced herself she could handle something devouring her was the same as his case.

After Philomena sat down, Gino stood up for the first time to share his story. As memories of his father's death, his battles with the mob, and the loss of two women exploded in his mind, he said, "Hello, my name is Gino, and I'm an addict."

1

GINO AND MICHELLE
One Year Earlier, Fall 1986

*D*uring the fall in New England, trees paint their leaves with brilliant reds and yellows. The leaves fall and cover the ground like a blanket soon after they peak. A deep breath can remind you that snow will soon fall. In the meantime, tourists swarm over New England like swallows returning to Capistrano, clogging highways and hotels in the hope of watching one of Mother Nature's most spectacular shows.

Gino Peterson reached across the bed and stroked the hair of the woman beside him. Despite his touch, she slept soundly. While she lay on her side, he was captivated by her rhythmic breathing. He admired her generous curves. Taking in the warmth of her body, he lingered for as long as he could.

Gino looked across the room at his state police uniform. First, he saw a Smokey Bear-type hat called a Stetson. The hat badge was gold and shined to a high gleam. The state police motto, "In the Service of the State," was engraved on the tri-angle-shaped emblem.

Gino would soon tuck a gray shirt and black tie into riding pants called breeches. The three-quarter-length jacket, called a blouse, with four large pockets and brass buttons, went over the shirt. Military-type epaulets topped each shoulder, and on the right and left upper arm was sewn the distinctive patch of the RI State Police; U.S. and RI flags crossed a red-and-black rendering of RI's distinct State House. Finally, the entire gray uniform was piped in red.

The most distinctive feature of the uniform was the cus-tom-made riding boots each trooper wore. A bootmaker took exact measurements of a trooper's ankle and calf to ensure the boots were comfortable enough to withstand a fifteen-hour workday.

The night before, his leather holster, cuff case, and belt had been polished to a high gloss. The holster was cross-drawn for Gino, meaning it was placed on his right side because he was left-handed. Right-handers wore the holster on their left side. In addition, a woven cord, a lanyard, was attached to the butt of the gun and the shoulder opposite the holster. Soon, Gino would dress in his uniform and report to his station, or, as they called it, the barracks.

Just three short years ago, he was a member of the RI State Police Intelligence Unit, considered by many to be the most desired assignment in the department. During his assignment, the state police convinced three mob associates to cooperate and testify. It was a bumpy road, but a guilty verdict was obtained using the trio's testimony. It appeared that justice had triumphed until the Intelligence Unit security detail led by Gino escorted cooperating witnesses Frank Martellini and Billy Franco from Superior Court, where a corrupt federal agent shot them dead.

After the ambush, Gino was transferred back to the uniform division. He would not be promoted or given choice assignments. His fellow troopers nicknamed him "Trooper for Life." Nothing, except a return to the Intelligence Unit, could heal Gino's broken spirit.

Gino's immediate supervisor and former lover, then sergeant and now demoted Corporal Michelle Urban, was also transferred from the unit to the demeaning role of Supervisor of the Evidence Room. The thing that had kept Gino and Michelle together, the state police and the job pressures, ultimately caused them to grow apart when they no longer shared a joint mission. When they drifted apart, Gino had floated into the arms of Renée.

Renée St. Pierre stirred and turned over; she looked toward Gino.

"Good morning, Trooper Peterson."

"Good morning, Professor St. Pierre."

While Gino had to prepare for his shift, Renée had to rise and begin her duties as professor of criminal justice at Regent Community College.

"Dibs on the shower," she jumped out of bed and ran into the bathroom.

Gino put his feet on the floor and sat on the edge of the
bed. He stretched and yawned and waited for his turn in the
shower.

2

FALLS CHURCH, VIRGINIA
Fall 1988

A security guard patrolled a warehouse in Falls Church, Virginia. In the dimly lit edifice, he moved slowly and deliberately. In the early morning, there was a graveyard-like atmosphere. He moved from station to station, wearing the dingy blue uniform of a rent-a-cop, a man with supposed authority but no real power and certainly no gun.

He was exhausted, the kind of exhaustion that hides behind your eyes and never leaves. Despite his efforts to stay in shape after his medical discharge from the Army, he had lost that battle long ago. His stomach hung over his belt like a waterfall, and the oval shape of his face was accentuated by gray hair that he parted on the side. Despite being only fifty-nine years old, he looked eighty.

When he looked in the mirror, he saw his father's face staring back at him, but he ignored it preferring to see himself as a young man. The silence in the cavernous space comforted Richard Douglas as he walked around. He welcomed the quiet after so much noise in his life.

A small key was firmly inserted into the round Simplex leather register case he wore over his shoulder like a large purse. Each stop was carefully planned to ensure the entire building was checked and guards did not sleep eight hours. In his past life, silence and boredom were alien concepts. He wondered how long he could keep up this charade. He didn't know if he'd be able to hide his true nature for much longer.

Douglas punched out at seven in the morning. A former cop, nicknamed Cookie, took over his Simplex ball and chain. A lingering smell of cigarettes and booze made Douglas turn his head quickly. Cookie took the Simplex from him and asked, "Hey, Douglas, you're not from around here, are you?"

Douglas stepped back to avoid the stinky breath that invaded his nostrils, but Cookie took it as a sign that Douglas didn't want to talk.

"It's just a simple question. I'm curious."

Richard Dexter was familiar with law enforcement due to his unconventional past. He harbored doubts about Cookie, as he had encountered numerous cops throughout his life. However Dexter was not who he purported to be. In truth, he was Richard Capelli, a former soldier in the New England Organized Crime family. Known as "Moon" due to his round face, he was presently under the protection of the U.S. Marshal's Witness Protection Program.

Cookie persisted, undeterred by Moon's snarky attitude. "I'm simply pointing out that despite my Southern accent, I pronounce my Rs correctly. It's CAR, not CAA," he emphasized.

Moon replied with a hint of sarcasm: "Well, excuse me, Colonel Sanders."

. . .

Moon put on his Members Only jacket and left Cookie behind as he stepped out into the dry breeze. His apartment was only a twenty-minute walk from the warehouse. As he walked, he took deep breaths of fresh air to rid his nose of Cookie's stench.

While in Falls Church, Moon took advantage of the city's diversions. His twenty-year-old 1966 Dodge Dart was not adorned with the bells and whistles he was accustomed to, so most of the time he walked. He was used to a better life, starting with a roomier vehicle like a Cadillac or a Lincoln Continental—those cars affectionately called Guinea Gondolas by the gangster world.

At just over two miles square, Falls Church was nick-named "The Little City." Most people who settled here worked in Washington, DC. It offered the atmosphere of a small town without the hustle and bustle of the big city.

Moon was amazed at the number of coffee shops in Falls Church, from national chains to locally owned businesses. He walked into his favorite, Colonial Coffee House, which was located in a three-story house. Looking across the hardwood floors, he noticed a half-wall covered in pictures of coffee. A bean farmer carried sacks on a miniature donkey, coffee beans, bags, and steaming mugs of coffee hung there. The aroma of coffee, the gods' nectar, filled the room. Pastries and bagels were displayed in a glass case.

Moon's favorite barista was tall and thin, not yet twenty years old. Despite his neat appearance, he had messy hair and a scruffy beard. In addition to his apron, he wore a pressed long-sleeve shirt with his name pinned to the chest.

Getting too close to anyone or frequenting the same place was a bad idea for Moon. One of his enemies could see him. For the twentieth time that week, he wished he had a piece in case someone tried to take a shot at him. However, owning a weapon was forbidden under the terms of the program he was in.

"Good morning, Richard. Is it the usual?" Kyle asked. Acne engulfed his face with a vengeance, leaving him self-conscious to the point where he couldn't make eye contact.

Moon replied, "I'm fine with that, Kyle."

"Large black coffee and a cinnamon raisin bagel with extra cream cheese are coming up. Richard, have a seat, and I'll bring it over."

At a table, Moon took in the buzz of people on a caffeine high. Moon thought, This is the best legal drug on the market.

"Here you go. Enjoy," Kyle said as he lingered at the table.

Every time someone called him Richard instead of Moon, it took a moment to register. To make up for any lag in the conversation, Moon started another conversation quickly.

"You're off to college soon, right?"

Kyle tucked his thumbs into the straps of his Colonial House apron. He said, "Well, I'm supposed to start at Lynchburg University, but I'm not sure about going."

"Why?"

"You know I love it around here. I got a good job. People know me, and my girl's here."

Moon saw doubt in his eyes. "Are you sure you want to give up college?"

"It has more to do with fitting in. I've been to campus, and it's nice. I get the feeling I will feel like a fish out of water."

"Son, I know the feeling," Moon said, and Kyle rushed back to work, too busy to understand what the hell that meant.

. . .

Two weeks later, Moon was on his way home from work when he decided to stop at the Colonial. He wasn't ready for bed yet, so he figured a half-caf coffee might help him decide whether to stay up for several more hours or hit the sack.

Moon was in line when he was alerted to someone he suspected was unsavory. Whether it was someone following him or a punk who thought he would be a soft touch to rob, Moon was always on the lookout. Life is a dangerous endeavor for everyone, but more so for a member of the Witness Protection Program. He had to keep his instincts intact.

The man had long, shoulder-length hair that was a mix of blond and gray. He estimated his age at thirty to thirty-five. His sweatpants and shirt were soiled, and dirty running shoes completed his outfit. Moon thought he looked like Lurch from *The Addams Family.* The only thing he did was stare at everyone.

Moon got up and walked behind the guy in line. If the guy tried to take him out, he would react. It might blow his cover, but survival would always come first.

The man did not react to Moon's movement. He was too busy looking at a young boy who was no older than ten years old. The boy had a mischievous face, blond hair, and freckles galore. Moon was reminded of Dennis the Menace by his goofy personality.

At the back of the shop was a small restroom—a toilet stall with a urinal and sink. The boy entered the bathroom, and the man followed him. Moon followed them in to see what was happening, sensing that something wasn't right.

Following the boy, the man entered the stall. He was alone with the boy after closing the door behind him. "Hey, mister, what are you doing here?"

"It's all right, little fella. I'm just checking on you. I'll help you unbutton your pants, just like your parents."

Moon heard the boy yell, "Leave me alone!"

Moon surprised the man by swinging the stall door inward, pinning him against it.

Moon looked at the boy, "Get the hell out of here, kid!"

The boy ran out with fear in his eyes and tears streaming down his cheeks. A fistful of the man's hair was in Moon's hands in a flash. "What were you thinking, asshole?"

"Hey man, what the hell are you doing? I was just trying to help the kid," he pleaded.

"Well, I'm here to teach you how to swim, Lurch."

Moon slid his left hand into the degenerate's long hair to secure it. As soon as he slammed him into the stall, the man screamed in pain. Moon grabbed him with one hand and punched him in the head and gut dropping him to the floor. He quickly followed it up by slamming his knee into the back of the man's neck, ensuring he could not move.

Grabbing him by the hair, Moon pulled him up and stuck his head in the toilet and flushed it several times. "OK, now breathe and hold, and now repeat. You're doing great, Lurch," Moon said. His prey begged for mercy between air gasps, but there would be no mercy on this day. He slumped to the floor after Moon's last punch landed between his legs. Moon looked down at the broken man with a smirk on his face. He spat on the ground and walked away without a second glance. The man lay there, alone and helpless, as the echoes of his cries faded into the bathroom stall. There were screams, then whimpers, and then silence. The man had drifted off into unconsciousness. His breathing was shallow, and a trickle of blood ran from the corner of his mouth onto the floor.

As Moon left the men's room, the customers lowered their heads and stared into their coffee cups. The cops were on their way, and they would want answers. Moon felt this was the last time he would ever visit the Colonial.

"What's the matter, Richard?" Kyle asked. "Is everything okay?"

Moon answered, "Everything's fine, but there's some shit on the floor in the men's room that needs to be cleaned up."

"Sure, right away," Kyle said. Moon left the store and saw the boy talking to his parents, who comforted him as they dealt with the confusion. Then, as a police cruiser approached the coffee shop, Moon smiled at the young man and walked away.

There it was on display for all to see, Moon's aggression and brutality that he had learned too well from the "life." It would continue to serve him well if he were to return to the mobster life.

3

MOON'S DOUBLE LIFE

oon walked the cold, damp streets of Falls Church. The weather wasn't good for hanging around outside, so he rolled up the collar of his thin jacket and headed home instead.

Living a life of boredom and normalcy made Moon feel like he was trapped in a *Twilight Zone* episode. He rented a furnished, one-bedroom apartment. Previously inhabited by workers for nearby companies, the building was a converted meat packing plant on the city's west side. Rents for a furnished apartment in the retrofitted building were reasonable.

His black boots slammed each stair as he walked up the Boston Back Bay-style stairs. Frustration and stubborn resignation drove each step harder than the last. He was sure no one had been in his apartment since the small piece of tape he had stretched between the bottom of the door and the frame wasn't broken.

Moon cautiously entered, scanning the dark environment to ensure that no one was hiding there, waiting to seek revenge on him. After turning on the lights, he proceeded down a small hallway and arrived at the kitchen with a dirty sink and cabinets surrounding a small window. The tiny bedroom had a twin bed and a small lamp on the nightstand. A battered bureau was pushed against the wall opposite a window.

Confident a hidden assailant wouldn't attack him, he sat down at the kitchen table. The scratches from a thousand previous renters scarred the surface, marking the shared desperation of their lives. He wondered how many others living a life of dull repetition had sat in this room trying to figure out why their lives went to shit. How many ever found a way out? Or never did? These thoughts were his only companions, and he grew tired of their presence.

Moon was sure he wasn't going to be killed that day, but he knew the day was coming when he couldn't take this mundane life any longer. As a former associate of the Raimondi crime family, he would always crave the status of being connected, not to mention his craving for the women who presented themselves for the taking just because someone was in the mob.

Once again, Moon considered starting a gambling operation in Falls Church or extorting Little Saigon restaurants and businesses. He knew that Vietnamese gangs ran the streets and would not like someone encroaching on their territory, however.

And even if he could live a life of crime in Virginia, it would not erase what ate at his core. He had been forced to leave the life he loved in shame, and he needed to redeem himself. He could only do that where his roots and heart lived. It was time for Moon to face reality. He needed more money and connections, and they were all back in Providence. It would be impossible for the mob to forget he had turned state's witness. So, his return had to prove he could give them what they have always wanted—money.

4

WITNESS PROTECTION

Moon received a phone call every Saturday at 10:00 a.m. from U.S. Marshal Jason Ryan. Moon was keenly aware that Ryan cared little about him as a person; he was making one of the many calls he had to make that day to ensure everything was in order with his charges.

"Hello," Moon said dryly in preparation for the ritual he endured every week.

"Hello, Mr. Douglas," Ryan asked. "How are you doing?"

"Fine, Mr. Ryan, all is well."

"Great, well then, I'll speak to you next week."

Moon had other plans for the call, however. Before Ryan hung up, Moon said, "It's time for me to get more money. I'm getting minimum wage at work, and you started sending me five hundred a week. Now it's only a hundred. That's barely enough for me to survive. Even if I meet someone cute, I can't take them out to eat. What kind of life is that?"

Ryan said with disdain, "Listen, Moon, the whole purpose of the program is for you to eventually become independent of government handouts. We'll continue to pay your rent if you're responsible, but you won't receive any extra cash. That's when guys like you get into trouble."

Moon was angry. "Come on, after all I did for the IU you're trying to treat me like some shithead?"

"Listen, I don't give a flying fuck what you did for the Intelligence Unit. You're in the program now. We are required to keep you safe. It's your responsibility to start a new life. Understood?"

Moon thought better of pressing the issue. Ryan's response just added to his desire to return to the mob. "Capisco," was Moon's reply.

"What?"

"I understand, I understand. Okay, okay," came Moon's reply.

"Goodbye, Mr. Douglas," Ryan hung up.

Moon slammed the receiver down. "Goodbye and kiss my ass, Mr. Ryan."

5

THE NATION'S CAPITAL

oon would occasionally visit DC to wander among the tourists and government workers. Ryan had warned him to stay out of the city because that increased the possibility that someone from his past could recognize him. However, he argued he had survived the streets of Providence and its wars by being cautious and not acting foolishly. Ryan, knowing what Moon said was true, relented.

Sometimes the most effective place to hide is out in the open. Moon occasionally noticed someone suspicious or a stranger with a particular look. When it happened, the hair on his neck stood up until he was sure he wasn't being stalked.

Looking around, he wondered if anyone knew they were in the company of a notorious mobster. But, of course, he hadn't intended it to unfold this way; it just happened. He had been in the wrong place at the wrong time, and now he was stuck. He just had to hope that his presence had gone unnoticed. He knew if he made one wrong move, this could be his last night alive.

The District appealed to Moon because it was an expanded version of Providence. Although there was no "Little Italy" in DC, restaurants serving Italian-American cuisine were popular in the city, and many Italian-Americans still lived here. In the early 1900s, Italian immigrants built the Holy Rosary Church at Third and F streets. When Moon visited the church every Easter and Christmas, he was brought back to his childhood on Federal Hill.

Moon's father, Giovanni, and mother, Patricia, were first-generation Italians. Giovanni worked in his father's butcher shop, while Patricia raised her two sons at home. For extra money, she tailored dresses for neighborhood women.

Moon was about twelve when he and his older brother, Peter, tried to steal some fruit from Enzo's fruit cart. Even though he was only five feet six inches tall, Giovanni towered over his sons.

"I want you to pay attention, boys. I will beat you with my belt until you cry for mercy if you steal again. Meanwhile, I want you to think about how you want to spend the rest of your lives." Giovanni spoke with a heavy Italian accent.

They relaxed a bit. "Blood is all over my apron from butchering. I do it ten hours a day, six days a week. It's more than blood. It's work, so your life will be better than mine. And your children's lives will be better than yours."

Even though they had not even actually stolen anything, Peter felt guilty and said, "Pops, we know how hard you and Mom work for us. I promise we will behave."

This was typical of their relationship. Peter was older and felt it was his duty to protect his younger brother. Moon often looked to his older brother for guidance and tried to take any opportunity to learn from him. But Moon himself wasn't so sure that pinching a piece of fruit needed to be treated like the end of the world. Despite the threat of the belt, Moon continued stealing and fighting. As he got older, he was arrested several times as a juvenile.

When his father returned home from work on the day of Moon's eighteenth birthday, Moon expected the family to have a meal and a birthday cake for him.

In contrast, when his father came in from work, he seemed somber, not angry, but resolute. He said, "Richard, wash up, then you go to the car."

Moon was thrilled. Oh, they're taking me out! he thought.

Standing in front of the car, he was surprised no one was there. Then, after a few minutes, Patricia and Peter appeared. Patricia clutched Peter to her bosom as tears rolled down her cheeks. Peter stood silently, and Moon stared back at them, wondering what was happening.

His father appeared with a small suitcase, handed it to Moon, and told him to get in the car. As they drove away, Moon waved at his family.

"Pop, Pop, what's going on?" Exhaustion and fear roiled him simultaneously.

"I will drive you to Fort Dix Army Base in New Jersey. When we get there, you're gonna enlist in the Army."

"The Army? I don't want to enlist in the Army."

"I'm afraid you are, son. Yesterday, I got a call from the judge handling your cases. He told me that because you are eighteen now, you had two choices: enlist or jail. You are not going to jail, understand?"

"Yes, sir," Moon replied, and they drove in silence for the remainder of the journey.

6

MOON JOINS THE AIRBORNE RANGERS
25 Years Earlier

After enlisting, Moon was sent to Fort Benning, Georgia, for basic training. He endured the training primarily out of pride. He hadn't forgiven his father for sending him there and wasn't trying to make his family proud by excelling in the service. He found that the better he did, the more he was left alone.

Robert Lee Montgomery was his drill instructor for the first half of Moon's training. Originally from Mississippi, he was a good ol' boy. He disliked Moon at once and rode him hard. His great-great-grandfather's plantation was literally the size of Rhode Island. So, he called him an "eye-talian from that shit stain of a state up north."

Robert Lee Montgomery was about five feet ten inches tall, with broad shoulders. He had buzzed his hair and wore the legendary brown felt campaign hat with the brim resting just above his eyebrows.

One day, when Montgomery gathered Moon's platoon, he asked them to fill out a dream sheet about their next training after basic. Unfortunately, Moon made a mistake in expressing interest in jump training.

"You want to do what, Oreo?" he asked. "Why would you want to jump out of a perfectly good plane? Did your Italian mama drop you on your head as a baby?"

"Sergeant Montgomery, I think I would be good at it."

"Oh, you do, Oreo? First, you talk funny and sound like a gangster. Second, you still need to get out of basic. And third, I don't like eye-talians."

"Sir, I'm sorry to hear that."

"Oreo, how often do I have to tell you not to call me sir? I'm not a goddamn officer. I work for a living." The sergeant turned around and walked away.

■ ■ ■

Moon escaped Montgomery after completing basic training and being sent to advanced infantry training. Sgt. Domenic Ruggeri, a Jersey native, was his drill instructor. His training was just as tough as Montgomery's, but it focused more on getting him ready for his first assignment.

Toward the end of the training, the unit gathered to hear from Ruggieri, who was also one of the "Black Hats" instructors who guided recruits through jump school.

Instead of a regulation cap, he wore a black baseball cap with a Master Parachutist badge attached. It was in stark contrast to the green camo uniform. Ruggieri was a tall, lanky soldier with the habit of swiping his nose as he talked. He had an angular face with deep-set eyes and ears that sprouted out of his head.

"Listen up. Some of you might be considering jump school, but I've seen your sorry asses on PT. You look like a bunch of monkeys trying to fuck a football. You ain't Ranger material."

While Moon prepared his application packet for Airborne School, he remembered that adding a little something might make Ruggieri consider his application favorably.

Moon called his brother because he always relied on him. "Peter, can you ship some meat and cheese from the Village market?"

"What do you need that stuff for?" Peter asked.

Moon replied, "I'm trying to get into jump school, and if I give some to my Italian DI, it might help my cause."

Peter sighed, "All right, Moon, anything else?"

"How about a couple of bottles of wine, maybe a red and a white?" Moon asked.

"All right, brother, I will send you a bottle of Salice Salento and a Verdeca," Peter replied.

"Thanks, fratello, you're the best. Gotta go," Moon hung up.

Moon delivered the packet and gifts his brother shipped to him to Ruggieri's quarters. Then, with a note of thanks, he placed them on his bunk. Ruggieri was quite appreciative, apparently, and the following week, Moon was enrolled in Fort Benning's three-week Basic Airborne Course (BAC).

▪ ▪ ▪

As he sat next to his fellow trainees, the roar of the C-130 cargo plane drowned out any chatter. This was Moon's first jump, and his mind raced to remember all he was taught to do once he left the plane.

When making an airborne jump, the objective was to come in low in the darkness of the night. The Army learned from WWII that soldiers were easy prey for the enemy as they floated to the ground. Rangers jumped at eight hundred feet, but recruits were required to complete five jumps at twelve hundred feet.

The bench Moon sat on was foldable aluminum with red nylon webbing. It was not exactly comfortable, but it was not made to be. Moon was focused on listening to the jump commands from the jumpmasters. When the jump light turned from red to green, it was time to go.

At twelve hundred feet above the ground, sixty-four trainees were about to jump. The jumpers repeated in their heads: maintain tight body position, prepare for a shock when the canopy opens, and check for other jumpers.

Though there were two parachute systems, main and auxiliary, on Moon—weapon, helmet, and gear pack—he was deathly afraid of the jump. Even though he felt ready, there was always a doubt that he would end up splattered on the ground. As he waited to make the jump, he struggled with the overwhelming fear of taking the leap. With every ounce of strength, he battled to suppress his terror and apprehension, willing himself to confront the daunting void below. But he also began to feel that maybe he had a purpose beyond his path prior to enlisting. Or, more accurately, being enlisted.

All sixty-four rose in unison on green and attached their clips to the anchor line cable. Looking toward the jumpmaster, Moon noticed the electric winch at his feet. A way in which a jumper could be retrieved in case of an emergency.

Moon did not like the thought of bouncing off the underbelly of the C-130 while being reeled back into the plane. Before he could think about it any longer, he jumped out of the plane's open door.

Moon felt the rush of air assaulting his body as he fell at over a hundred miles per hour. He forced himself to concentrate on counting: thousand and one, thousand and two, thousand and three, thousand and four. PULL.

When the chute opened, the chaos of a sky filled with jumpers shocked his senses. Moon followed his training and turned to the right (never to the left) to avoid colliding with another jumper. It was hell on earth before the chute opened. It was like being dropped from a bridge tied to a bungee cord. When his chute was deployed, heaven opened its arms. As he floated toward Earth, he was at peace. Everything slowed down suddenly, and he wished the descent would last forever.

Moon hit the ground and rolled. He quickly wrapped up his chute and avoided jumpers landing all around him. He was relieved that he had survived his first jump and prayed that all the jumps he faced would be just as benign.

Moon completed his training and graduated in an official ceremony at Ft. Benning. He was assigned to the 82nd Airborne.

Following the official ceremony, an unofficial ceremony took place in the barracks.

The controversial practice known as "Blood Wings" has been a long-standing tradition among some members of the Army, despite the disapproval of the higher-ups. To pass this rite of passage, each individual must expose their bare chest while their fellow graduates hammer the airborne wings into their flesh. For Moon, the experience was excruciating, but he persevered through the pain, aided only by the numbing effects of alcohol. Despite the urge to scream out in agony, he kept himself composed by gritting his teeth and taking swigs from a bottle of Tequila.

Moon made twelve jumps over the next two years, each as frightening and chaotic as the last. At twenty, he felt like a rubbery Gumby, bouncing back from minor injuries.

It was after Moon's last jump that his Army career came to an end. His main chute failed to deploy, and he descended too quickly. Fear gripped him: fear of dying, fear of the pain of hitting the ground, fear of never seeing his family again. He was so scared of the unknown that he was almost paralyzed with terror. As he descended further, however, he pushed his fear of death aside, concentrating instead on his training and following the steps they had taught him.

"The auxiliary, pull the auxiliary chute, you shithead!" he screamed into the rush of air that seized his words and pushed them back down his throat. Moon didn't remember hitting the ground, only waking up in the hospital. His secondary chute could not slow him down enough to prevent broken bones and internal injuries. He spent two months in the hospital. After recovering, he was medically discharged.

When he returned to Providence, the life of a gangster was all that appeared to be waiting for him. But first, he had to earn everyone's respect. And more important, their trust. He was rumored to have betrayed the Mafia code by joining the service. The Mafia comes first—before your family, before the government. He had to prove he was worthy and would never cross them again by swearing loyalty to any outside organization. He had to show that he wanted to be one of them and that the Army had shown him the legitimate life was not for him.

Initially, he was assigned mundane and tedious tasks such as collecting betting slips and making payments to loan sharks. However, he found himself particularly drawn to Bobo Detroia and his gang. With his exceptional talent for gambling, he was soon able to manage the entire book for the Detroia crew. His astute business acumen and gambling skills helped him establish himself as a prominent member of the criminal family, earning him a reputation as a shrewd and valuable asset to the organization.

7

GINO'S ROAD TO ADDICTION
Fall 1988

Gino had managed to remain in touch with a few colleagues from the Intelligence Unit, including Det. Lou Reynolds, his mentor and friend. In all aspects of Gino's life and work, he consulted Lou for advice.

They discussed Gino's issues as they lifted weights at the North Kingstown Fitness Center. Initially, he sought Lou out because he wanted to climb the organizational ladder. Now, most of their discussions focused on Gino regaining his reputation and getting another chance at the Intelligence Unit.

During a workout with Lou about a month after Gino started living with Renée, he was doing a bent-over row when he heard something pop. Gino tried ice and Advil for a few days, but the pain persisted.

Gino called his GP, Dr. Jeff Winters, who arranged for him to see Dr. Ariel Birnbaum, a well-known orthopedic surgeon. Gino met him in his office at Rhode Island Hospital. A nurse placed him in an exam room and asked him to wear a gown he had no idea how to tie. After about ten minutes, Dr. Birnbaum entered the room. The doctor was tall, taller than Gino, maybe six feet four inches. Light brown hair was parted on one side and swept across his head to the opposite ear. His features were soft and pleasing. Gino felt immediately relaxed.

Dr. Birnbaum was impeccably dressed. He wore a heavily starched white lab coat, an off-white shirt and blue-striped tie. After an exam where Gino was required to demonstrate his range of motion, which was relatively poor, the doctor jotted down some notes in his file.

"Mr. Peterson, I'm planning to send you for a CAT scan, but I'm pretty sure I know what's going on." His voice was a combination of respect and consolation.

"I think you have a bulging disc at L3, which is one of the parts of the spine that allows us to bend at the trunk. In your case, the disc that cushions the space between L3 and L4 is swollen and pressing on the nearby nerve."

"As you probably know, I'm a state trooper, and I'd like to get back to work as soon as possible."

"I understand completely. I'd like to send you for the scan and will call you with the result. After that, I will send you to physical therapy, which should resolve the problem. In the meantime, no more weightlifting. You must rest so that you will heal."

"Can you give me something for the pain?" Gino asked.

"I will give you a prescription for Vicodin. It's a powerful medication. Please don't drive or drink alcohol when you're taking them. Take one pill every twelve hours until the pain is bearable, and then switch to Tylenol."

"Thank you, Doc! I'll do that."

"You can get dressed now. Hand this slip to the front desk, and here's your script for Vicodin."

Dr. Birnbaum turned and headed out the door. When he reached it, he turned to Gino. "One more consideration, Mr. Peterson, Vicodin is an opioid that can become addictive. So only take it as prescribed."

"No problem. I understand."

Gino dressed, stopped at the desk, scheduled his first session, and took the script.

8

MICHELLE'S FALL FROM GRACE

*M*ichelle remembers her first day as a state police custodian of evidence. She was toured by Sgt. Bill Elbert, her immediate supervisor. Elbert, a veteran detective, supervised all detectives. A robust two-hundred-and-thirty pounds, he stood about five feet ten. He wore a corduroy suit in a dull brown. His hair was wiped away from his brown eyes and back to the top of his head. His hair always seemed to win the constant battle of staying off his forehead. Michelle thought his eyes belied his crusty exterior.

The state police's evidence room was in the basement of the headquarters building in the town of Scituate. All important evidence was brought here, and the room filled the entire basement. Battleship gray walls welcomed all visitors.

The office equipment was so outdated that it looked like it belonged on the set of *MASH*, the classic American TV series. The computer monitor was bulky. The printer was painfully slow and noisy. All in all, the office equipment was in dire need of an upgrade.

A chain-link fence stretched from the bottom of the counter to the ceiling, covering the wall-to-wall counter. A Dutch door led to rows of shelving containing evidence and case files. The shelves were stacked high with guns, drugs, knives, stolen goods, and crime scene evidence.

Seeing Michelle's stunned expression, Elbert said, "I know this isn't the best assignment or office, but—"

Michelle cut him off with, "I know what you're going to say because I hear it behind my back all the time. I couldn't handle living evidence, my witnesses, so now I better try dead evidence."

Elbert shrugged. He showed her how evidence was exchanged through an opening in the Dutch door cage. Elbert said, "Keeping track of the evidence shows it was always secure. The court must be assured that from street to courtroom no one has access to the evidence other than those authorized. You learned all this shit in the academy, but I must tell you."

He then showed her how evidence numbers and descriptions were entered into a hefty, bound book. Additionally, the arrestee's vitals were added. The outcomes of the cases were also recorded as well as any sentence assigned after a guilty plea. When the court ordered evidence destroyed or stolen goods returned to owners, it was noted in the book as well. All other activities related to the case were reflected in the ledger, including any court orders or subpoenas. The book became a comprehensive record of the case.

"It's almost 1988. Has anyone ever thought about computerizing this system?" Michelle asked.

The state police ledger was established in 1925. A meticulous handwritten entry was made by the evidence custodian. Elbert pondered for a moment. "I wasn't around in 1925, but I'm sure the administration felt it worked then, and it still does now. We've always done it that way."

Michelle did not respond but only noted to herself that while change is uncomfortable for everyone, it is especially unwelcome in law enforcement.

Sgt. Elbert walked away, "Good luck, Corporal. I'll be upstairs if you have questions. You're a smart girl. You'll figure it out."

"Girl? Did you just call me girl? It sounds like you've been around since 1925," she muttered under her breath.

She glanced around the room. As she breathed in deeply, she paused for a moment to consider how her once-promising career had crumbled. She was now a glorified clerk in an ocean of crime's byproducts. Memories of the murder of two protected witnesses washed over her like the odor of the rotting marijuana in the evidence room. If those witnesses were still alive, her relationship with Gino would have continued. Three years ago, Michelle's career was not the only casualty. After searching her whole life for love, she had lost that too.

After the murders, she and Gino had lost their way of speaking to each other with kindness. Sarcastic comments escalated, then became an icy silence. Finally, they both realized that what they had experienced killed their romance as thoroughly as the bullets killed their witnesses.

9

THE GINO AND RENÉE ROMANCE

usic started blaring from the clock radio at 5:45 a.m. It was too early in the morning for the DJ to be so hyper as he babbled about the weather and traffic. Most likely, it was caffeine-fueled energy. Gino groaned and rolled over in bed, determined to get some more sleep. With a heavy sigh, he reached over and turned off the clock radio.He twisted his large frame toward the floor and dropped his feet onto the floor. He remembered being in the academy and the instructor yelling at everyone to put their feet on the deck every morning at 6:00 a.m. He rubbed the sleep from his eyes as he prepared to face the day. He tried to quietly get to the bathroom before waking Renée up. It would only take him fifteen minutes to shower and shave. He had been stripped of the notion that getting ready took a long time at the state police academy.

Ready for the day now, Gino decided to bring Renée some coffee in bed. She was just as striking as the first time he ever laid eyes on her when she worked for the attorney general's office. They had become reacquainted, or perhaps really acquainted for the first time, when Gino took a course Renée offered as part of his Criminal Justice degree program.

Located in Warwick, the college was in the middle of the state. There was only one building, a concrete colossus devoid of architectural beauty. An above-ground bomb shelter on steroids. Gino entered room 4128 for Criminal Law on the first day of classes in September. As Renée entered the class, she gave him a nod of recognition and introduced herself to the others. Renée St. Pierre explained her expectations for the class, but Gino and the other cops focused on her appearance. She wore a silk blouse with pearl buttons, the first two of which were open. The outfit was completed with a blue blazer and a short skirt.

Coal-black hair flowed to her shoulders and was parted in the middle. Renée's hair was longer than he remembered. Occasionally, she would curl a strand around her finger in an unconscious gesture. His stomach churned with excitement, and he felt his face warm as he got lost in her blue eyes. It had been years since he had seen Renée, and he was overwhelmed by the sudden attraction he felt.

At the end of the first class, she gathered her papers and placed them in a leather case. Gino approached the podium cautiously, lingering for a few moments.

"Hello, Renée."

"I thought that was you, Gino."

"Could we grab a cup of coffee and catch up?" He was visibly nervous, and his voice cracked a bit. "It's been a while."

Renée looked at him warmly, a look he hadn't expected. Gino remembered her as a demanding prosecutor who didn't waste time on unnecessary matters. She was different somehow now, as if Regent College had softened her harsh exterior.

Gino found an empty high-top table in the coffee shop. He noticed students studying in soft beanbag seats as he walked over to place his order. Six vending machines lined up like toy soldiers offered fine cuisine and drinks.

It was black coffee for Renée and sugary tea for the macho trooper.

For the first few minutes, they sat in relative silence. Then, after exchanging pleasantries, she asked Gino a question that seemed oddly pointed.

"How's Michelle doing?"

Gino investigated his cup for answers. "I guess you didn't know this, but we're not together anymore. She was demoted and transferred from the unit after Marty and Billy were killed. Our relationship took a toll when I was booted out too."

"I'm sorry to hear that. I thought you two were really going to make it." Renée's words were conciliatory, but there wasn't any disappointment in her voice.

"I guess it just wasn't meant to be. My mom always asks what happened, but I have little to say because I don't know how it went sour so fast," Gino said.

"Gino, I'm sorry to cut you short, but I have another class in ten minutes."

"Of course, sorry." At that moment, Gino felt he needed more of this, more time with her. So, as they stood to leave, he said, "Do you think we could do this again, maybe even get a drink or have dinner?"

She replied quickly: "Of course."

Off she headed to her next class, and he wondered if this could be the start of something, or if she was just being kind to a wounded puppy.

10

ROMANCE AND VICODIN

The occasional coffee progressed to dating somewhat seamlessly. During those dates, they engaged in the talk of two people in their early thirties who had no time for mindless chitchat.

Gino took her on their first official date to Twin Oaks Restaurant, which was famous for its exceptional food and well-crafted drinks. People from all walks of life came to dine there, including the elites of Rhode Island. Over two large slices of veal parmigiana and a bottle of the house red, they started learning more about each other.

"When we last knew each other, I remember your fellow detectives gave you a hard time about the Yankees, right?"

"Look, one of the hardest things about living in RI is being a Yankees fan. I'm surrounded by Red Sox fans. They don't let me forget about it and dump on the Yanks every chance they get. I don't care because my mom's family loved the Yankees. DiMaggio, Rizzuto, and Berra were Italian. Everyone had to root for them, which started my obsession with baseball!"

Gino drove her home after they left the restaurant. During the ride, both were quiet with the glow of a good meal and several glasses of wine. To keep the high going, Gino took a Vicodin he had left over from a recent back injury. His emotions were already running high, and now he wondered just how good he could feel. Gino knew it was wrong, but he was in bliss and didn't want the moment to end.

Over time, Gino's body would begin to develop a tolerance to the Vicodin, so he needed more and more to get the same feeling. When he eventually realized that he had a problem, he was in too deep to stop.

Gino walked Renée to the door of her apartment, where they had an awkward first kiss. Gino's adrenaline surged again. "I'd like to see you again."

Renée kissed his forehead as she held his face in her hands. "I expect we will be spending a lot of time together, so yes, again and again and again." She kissed his cheeks and lips gently.

Eventually, they became inseparable. Most nights they ended up cooking food at Gino's or Renée's and enjoying copious amounts of alcohol. The first time they made love, they listened to *Pet Sounds* by the Beach Boys on Gino's record player. Then, when the record played its last song, the needle scraped along the smooth vinyl. As the music faded away, they lay still in each other's embrace, eyes closed. They spoke no words. In that moment, they were completely at peace with one another and the world around them. They felt a deep connection that surpassed the need for words, and all their worries and troubles seemed to slip away. All that mattered was they were together.

After a year of dating, they became tired of living in two places. They lived only twenty minutes apart, but in Rhode Island, any trip over ten minutes was considered a journey. In addition, there was no guarantee that the drive would take twenty minutes. What Rhode Island lacks in distance is made up for with potholes and winding roads. The couple moved into their new apartment in October. He said goodbye to Mrs. Ricci, his widowed landlord, and his $400 monthly rent.

11

GINO'S RELATIONSHIP WITH
HIS MOM

Gino cringed at one thing. His stomach began to churn at the thought of telling his Italian mother, Teresa Pompigna, now Peterson, that he was going to live with a woman outside the bonds of marriage. Gino thought he would rather pull out his hair one strand at a time than talk to her about Renée.

Renée told Gino she didn't have to ask anyone's permission at thirty-five. Her parents were in their late sixties and retired. Having sold the family pharmacy, they had moved to geriatric nirvana, a place called Florida.

Renée knew they trusted her judgment and would support her if she wanted to live with Gino. However, Renée was surprised that a thirty-five-year-old man would need his mother's permission to live with someone.

"Renée, it's not permission. It's more like approval. We have a different kind of relationship. No matter how old, every Italian boy always goes to his mama when he's in trouble or must make a big decision."

Gino tried to laugh it off but then dove into a deeper explanation. "After we lost my dad, all we had was each other. My mom still lives in the same second-floor tenement where she was born. Every day, she goes to Mass at Holy Ghost Church, the same church where she received the sacraments. She's worked in the same bakery for over thirty years."

"Thirty years in the same place?" Renée's voice was tinged with disbelief.

"I believe she stays there because it is set up like the café where she grew up in Sava. The dining area has four tables along a long bar-like counter. The customers stop in on their way to work just as they do in Italy for a quick espresso and cornetto," Gino explained.

Renée interjected, "Enough waffling, let me know why you need her permission."

Gino now had to explain the unexplainable, "There is something between an Italian mother and her son that I can't explain."

"Try," Renée said.

"I think Italian culture places a strong emphasis on family values. Sons are taught to respect and appreciate their mothers, who are viewed as a source of comfort and security."

Renée looked at Gino and saw fear in his eyes. "Gino, this is ridiculous. You mean to tell me she doesn't want you to be happy?"

He knew his mother wanted him to be happy, but not with anyone but Cpl. Michelle Urban. Teresa was still disappointed that Gino and Michelle had split up. When Gino started dating Renée, Teresa told Gino that Michelle, not Renée, was the one for him. Gino disagreed and told his mother that he was happy with Renée. Teresa was unconvinced, but eventually accepted that Gino had made his decision. She hoped that Gino would find the same happiness he had with Michelle in his new relationship.

"Look, I'll give you an example of how protective she is of me. A year ago, one of the mobsters I helped put away was released on parole. She called me because she feared he would try to get back at me. Like in *The Godfather*, she told me, when they shot the policeman.

"Jokingly, I told her not to worry because my landlady starts my car every morning. The phone went silent for about ten seconds. Then she says, 'Oh, that's good,' and hangs up."

They laughed, and Renée told him, "Then go see her and plead your case, Trooper!"

12

THE CONVERSATION

lthough Gino drove with a hefty dose of apprehension to his mom's house, he was relieved that the drive from the apartment in Cranston to the Federal Hill section of Providence did not take long. While the radio of his Jeep Wrangler blasted out tunes from the local FM station, Gino's anxiety melted away as he enjoyed the brief and pleasant drive.

He climbed the stairs to her second-floor apartment and approached the door. After three knocks, he heard her shuffling toward it. The familiar shuffle slowed with each passing year.

"Who is it?" Teresa asked.

He answered, "It's me, Mom."

"Oh, Gino, wait while I get the door," she replied.

She struggled with the deadbolt he installed for her safety; her arthritis-riddled fingers made it difficult. She opened the door after the bolt clicked into place.

Gino's smile broadened as Teresa came into view. Her smooth skin and clear eyes showed she was aging gracefully as she approached her sixty-fifth birthday. Brown hair with brilliant streaks of gray rested gently on her shoulders.

Standing an inch or two below five feet, she reminded Gino of one of the munchkins from *The Wizard of Oz*. It was a movie that his parents watched with him every year. At the end of the movie, they would ask what he had learned, and he would say, "There's no place like home."

Teresa wore a black cotton dress with a recurring white swirl and an apron. In the living room, an episode of *Golden Girls* was playing. She smiled a mother's smile, then waved her hand, motioned him in, and tossed the moppine (hand towel) over her shoulder with the other.

She greeted him with a hug and kisses on both cheeks. "My Gino, come, come into the house. Do you want something to eat? I just fried up some meatballs. I know they're your favorite."

Gino remembered eating them as a young boy. His mother would hand him one on a fork. Each was carefully fried in olive oil and seasoned with oregano and garlic. The smell alone would cause him to salivate, but today, his stomach was in no mood for food—not at least until he spoke to her about moving in with Renée.

"I can make you a sandwich in no time," Teresa said.

"No thanks, just something to drink. Water's fine," he said.

"Water, are you all right? You're not sick, are you?" Her hand went to his forehead, "You're not warm. I'm going to pour you a glass of wine."

Gino relented, "Fine, Mom. I'll have a glass of wine."

She reached under the kitchen cabinet and pulled out a gallon jug of homemade wine. She took out two jelly jars and filled them about halfway. Teresa placed them on her tiny kitchen table, which was covered by a tablecloth. The pattern of large wooden spoons and Chianti bottles was covered by a large piece of plastic.

Teresa waited until Gino took a sip. "This is good. Who made it?"

"Do you remember Mr. Lombardo? He lived on the first floor with his wife and elderly father. Well, after his father died, he bought a house in Johnston. He still comes back to the Hill to go to the bakery and market, and when he does, he drops off wine to his former neighbors."

Gino thought for a second. "Wait, was his father the old man who walked around the neighborhood, and when kids approached him, he barked like a dog?"

"That's the one. I felt sorry for him. All the kids, including you, teased him. You know the reason he barked was because he didn't speak English. He was probably trying to play with you and your friends."

"Hey, Mom, we were just kids. We didn't mean any harm. Anyway, how are things at the bakery?"

"Fine, I still enjoy going in, if only for the smells. When I breathe them in, they remind me of my childhood in Italy." Then, after a few more minutes of small talk about how he was doing and how she was doing, he decided to go for it and tell her.

"Mom, I wanted to talk to you about Renée and me. We're going to move in together."

When he said Renée, she put her glass down and smoothed out the tablecloth. As her hands moved across the table, she took a deep breath. Gino had seen her do this many times when giving her opinion on something he wanted to do.

"I don't understand why you would live with someone before you get married. Hopefully, you will get married someday, but if you do marry this girl you have to ask yourself—is this the person I want to spend the rest of my life with?" Teresa pleaded.

"It may seem rushed, but we want to be together. Are you sure that your feelings about Renée have nothing to do with Renée but have to do with Michelle?" Gino said.

"What do you mean?" she said.

Gino said softly, "I know you still don't understand or accept that Michelle and I are not together, but it was for the best."

She looked at him with love and the sternness he had come to accept and rely upon when he needed to hear what was best, not what felt right for him.

"You are a grown man, and I am very proud of everything you have accomplished. I pray every day for your safety. I know that your father looks down on you and is very proud. You are someone who knows right from wrong. A man who knows what commitment means and that life without commitment is a boat without a rudder. Now if you feel you need to commit to Renée, that's what you should do. I love you, Gino, and I always will. I pray you're making the right decision."

13

GINO PATROLS AND REMEMBERS
Winter 1989

The following day, Gino was awakened by the sound of his flip phone dancing on the nightstand. He reached for the phone and uttered a groggy hello.

"Peterson? Lieutenant Lemoi. You're on the desk this morning, so get your ass in gear and get here ASAP. I want to send O'Hearn home early."

"Right away, Lieutenant." The line went dead before he finished.

Awakened by the call, Renée asked, "What's up?"

"I just got assigned to the desk."

"The desk?" she said inquisitively. "They're giving you a desk job?"

Gino explained that "the desk" was a term used by troopers for being assigned to what most departments would call dispatch. Gino would spend the first five hours of his fifteen-hour shift answering calls and dispatching fellow troopers.

He would take reports from people coming to the barracks to report all manner of mayhem. Hope Valley Barracks, where he was stationed, was in a rural area that had two state parks.

Because of the rural nature of the area, many people stopped at the barracks for information. Directions to the Narragansett Indian Dovecrest restaurant were frequently requested. Exeter's tribal grounds made it difficult to find.

Many people traveled from all over the country to eat buffalo steak, venison, rabbit stew, and the show's star, Johnnycakes. *The New York Times* even called Dovecrest's Johnnycakes "the best in the world."

Gino tried them once but wasn't impressed. Gino wondered how Native Americans survived on what tasted to him like gruel, but these cornmeal flatbreads were a staple of Native Americans' diets.

Gino rolled out of bed, and Renée pulled the covers over her head hoping to catch another hour before she had to teach her first class.

Renée peeked out from the covers and watched Gino as he climbed into his uniform, "My goodness, don't we look dashing," Renée teased.

Despite being stared at, Gino continued to dress, saying, "You know I can put it on for you at any time?"

Renée feigned a sigh, "Now that's an offer a girl would find hard to refuse."

Troopers did not wear badges; instead, a small piece of black fabric with red trim was worn over the right breast. They called it the badge number board. The fabric was the same as that used to make the epaulets, and it was sewn into the uniform.

Each trooper was responsible for placing their gold badge numbers on the board. Gino's two and eight were pushed through the fabric at holes precisely measured and opened with an ice pick.

Gino's number, twenty-eight, was not only a way to identify him but also his identity. He would wear it his entire career and only surrender it when he retired. Then it would be passed on to a freshly minted recruit.

Using the palms of his hands, he tipped the front of his Stetson just above his eyebrows and secured the back with a small leather strap that clung to the nape of his neck. Gino looked in the mirror to ensure that his uniform was perfect. Large brown eyes staring back at him. Gino's prominent nose and eyes were proportionately spread across his face. A shock of gray skirted the temples of his short, cropped hair.

His father died when he was thirty years old, close to his own age. Both seemed to be in the prime of their lives. When a father dies violently at an early age, the trauma is multiplied tenfold. Thus, Gino was left to grieve with his mother and had to grow up quickly to provide emotional support to her. He also had to take over many of the responsibilities his father had handled. Gino had a lot of questions that he wanted his father to answer. Questions he knew would go unanswered.

Gino's dad was a loving man with flaws like any other man. In addition to working in a jewelry factory, he worked a second job as a janitor to support his family. Unfortunately, his father, Albert, liked to gamble, which sometimes led to financial difficulties. During those times, Gino and Teresa were harassed endlessly by bill collectors.

Before his father died, his dad needed a new car, but getting credit was difficult. So, Joe, Albert's nephew, who worked at a car dealership, arranged the financing for a used car.

Reliving the scene, Gino closed his eyes.

"Unc, the car is all set and ready to be driven, but my sales manager wants to talk to you before you leave."

"I appreciate you helping me out, Joe," Albert replied.

The sales manager reminded Gino of the gangsters who hung out on the corner of his neighborhood. This short man's belly swallowed his belt and waist. He slicked back his sandy blond hair into a pompadour. He had black marble-like eyes with beady pupils. The manager's jaw had an odd shape as if it had been broken and never set correctly. He drooled, and he sprayed spit at anyone nearby.

The sales manager approached and got into Albert's face. "Listen to me, Peterson, the only reason you're getting this car is because of your nephew, Joe. He's my number one salesman. So, I'm telling you that you better make the payments on time. Do you understand?"

Gino couldn't believe anyone would talk like that to his father. The manager's admonishment embarrassed him, and he stood there frozen.

While his father nodded and walked away, Gino could see that no matter how tough he was, he was humiliated and defeated in front of his son.

They rode home in silence after the joy of a new car ride was taken away. In retrospect, Gino regretted not speaking up for his father. What kind of jerk speaks that way to his hero?

He could fill a library with all the things he wished he had said to the manager.

* * *

Gino stepped into a clear winter's day and fired up his Plymouth 440 Fury equipped with a police package. Heavy-duty suspension secured the car to the road, and a powerful battery ensured it would start under any conditions.

Gino remembered that when he first became a trooper, the cruiser had just one red light, affectionately known as the gumball; today's cruiser, by contrast, was awash in red, white, and blue lights. Strobes had also been added to the light show. The intention was to break down the will of a prospective perpetrator, to get them off balance by overloading the senses. It tended to make even hardened criminals a little more pliable.

When he started the engine, the roar was as soothing to him as a mother's lullaby to a baby. Gino turned on the radio to the local sports station. They were interviewing Oakland A's pitcher Rollie Fingers, famous for his waxed handlebar mustache and skill as a relief pitcher.

The A's were coming off a World Series loss to the LA Dodgers in October, but today, sports were not at the forefront. Instead, Fingers was talking about the earthquake that struck the Oakland area just before the start of game three. He described it as a surreal experience and was thankful everyone in the stadium got out safely.

The station broke for commercials as Gino guided the cruiser to Route 95. Scattered among the steady stream of drivers were criminals. Their purpose was to transport all manner of contraband and stolen cars. Fugitives were escaping their last crime and hoping to outrun the law.

At the academy, Gino was taught that almost every crime involves a vehicle. Given that lesson, Gino and his fellow troopers scoured the highway for their criminal prey. But in Gino's world, he was an earthquake that opened the road and swallowed his prey whole.

14

MOON'S TRIP TO DC BECOMES DANGEROUS

efore returning to RI, Moon had some unfinished business. As a member of the Witness Protection Program, he was obliged to obey the law. Well, try anyway.

Prostitutes were Moon's greatest vice. Although Moon was arrested multiple times for this offense when he was back in Providence, he never served any jail time. In his view, this was a minor issue compared to other crimes, and no one was being harmed. To avoid any serious consequences, Moon used his money and connections.

Moon never entered a long-term relationship when he was on the streets. Now that he was in the program, committing to a woman was even more dangerous. If he really committed to someone—even fell in love with them—then he would have to lead a double life. He could keep that up for a while, but not forever. But it was either that or he would have to explain where he came from, where he grew up, and how he ended up in Virginia. Would that cause the right woman to stay with him and protect him? He had never been in such a relationship, and it felt daunting to even try.

Besides, what would be the attraction for a woman? The dashing security guard uniform or maybe the drab one-bedroom apartment? The lack of money?

And so, Moon was driven to the sex workers in DC to quench his thirst for intimacy. At the Falls Church Metro Station, he would take the train to DC, then the Red Line to Rhode Island Ave. Finally, he would walk along New York Avenue where prostitutes plied their trade in front of the city's iconic row houses.

Moon was particularly fond of Svetlana, a tall, blond woman with high cheekbones. Her hair was styled with lots of hairspray and teased to add volume. She usually wore a short dress that barely covered her legs, which she complemented with boots. Her dark makeup and red lips added to her overall look.

After several "dates," Moon learned she had been brought to the US from Croatia. Svetlana paid $5,000 to a coyote for transportation to America and a job. Instead, she was beaten, drugged, and then turned out on the streets by a pimp named Dmitri.

Svetlana's "mobile office" was a beat-up Chevy Vega parked in a dark alley where love was doled out in twenty-dollar blowjobs and straight lays for fifty. If you preferred not to navigate around the gear shift knob in the front seats of the Vega, a nearby room could be rented by the hour. Svetlana charged one hundred dollars for the move indoors.

For the last year, Moon had seen her once a month, usually after getting paid on Fridays. That ended one night when he met her on the avenue. The weather was cold, so Moon asked her to go to the hotel with him.

Moon paid the clerk forty dollars for an hour. The clerk looked like he was on amphetamines. Throughout the check-in process, he talked nonstop; Svetlana was oblivious to what was happening.

Moon paid Svetlana one hundred dollars once they entered the room, and he planned to tip her at the end of their hour-long meeting. However, he sensed something wasn't right as he undressed. Svetlana's hand shook as she folded back the sheets, and she kept her head down. Maybe she's just high, Moon thought.

Moon was in the buff as he climbed into bed. In a bra and panties, Svetlana hesitated to follow him. A clap of thunder sounded as the door burst open. With a gun in hand, her pimp, Dmitri, rushed into the room with bad intentions.

He was a small man built like a Russian weightlifter from the Olympics. A mass of muscles upon which a head sat. His nose spread across his face, eyes dark and lifeless. Beyond those eyes, evil and cruelty lurked. Dimitri was wearing a black tee shirt and sweatpants. A large gold chain hung from his neck.

Moon was just escaping the initial shock when Dimitri said, "Get the fuck out of bed." The accent was right out of central casting for a Russian bad guy.

"All right, all right," Moon said, "What do you want?"

"Money and credit cards." He spoke with a surprisingly high-pitched voice.

"I don't have any credit cards, you dumb fuck. The money is in the wallet."

Dmitri was about to strike gold. After paying for the room and Svetlana, Moon still had two hundred and fifty from his paycheck. With Dmitri's snub nose .38 pointed at his head, Moon needed little persuasion to hand over the wallet.

Dmitri rifled through it, took the money, and tossed the wallet in the corner. Dmitri slapped Svetlana a couple of times. It was the most unconvincing performance since Saddam Hussein tried to convince the world that Kuwait was part of Iraq.

Dimitri then pointed the gun at Svetlana's head. "Get the fuck out of here, whore. You come back here again, and I'll put a bullet in your gahlavah."

As Svetlana grabbed her clothes, she ran. Dmitri ordered Moon to lie flat on the mattress. Holding his gun against Moon's head, he pushed his face into the bed.

Dmitri spit as he talked, and Moon could feel the droplets hitting his head, "Now you lie here and don't move for ten minutes, understand?"

"Understood." Moon managed to get the word out despite his collapsed face.

Dimitri left the room. Moon lay on the mattress thinking, I just got robbed because this Ruskie was probably still pissed about the "Miracle on Ice."

15

MOON FINDS SVETLANA
Winter 1989

It had been several weeks since that fateful encounter with Dmitri. Fall was about to give up her grip and make way for winter, but not before she delivered an arctic blast to the Northeast. Winter was one cold-hearted bitch. Moon blew warm breath into his gloveless hands as he found a recessed doorway on New York Ave. in DC.

Moon wore jeans, a flannel shirt, a tan Dickey work jacket, and construction boots. A rolled-up ski mask covered his head, and a pint of Smirnoff vodka and a blackjack were tucked inside his jacket pockets. He started looking for Svetlana at one in the morning. Moon would take his revenge tonight.

The streets were a symphony of noises. One could hear the roar of cars as they sped away from approaching sirens. The screams of lovers' arguments leaked out of closed windows.

Prostitutes walked up and down their assigned territory. Customers drove around in a fever, anxious to make a purchase like shoppers on Black Friday, searching for the right date for the night, escaping reality before returning to their wife and kids.

When Moon spotted her on the outskirts of Chinatown, it was 2:00 a.m. She was right where he expected her to be, as her routine was familiar to him. Svetlana wore knee-high red boots and a wide-lapel blue blouse. Unbuttoned, her tiny breasts were exposed to the frigid air. To protect herself from the cold, she wore a faded and stained white bunny jacket.

When Moon approached her, Svetlana recognized him and recoiled in fear. The cigarette she smoked fell from her lips, and she took several steps back. Then, she raised her hands, reached up to her puffed hair, and pulled out a large hair pick with sharpened points. Svetlana was going to fight against the beating that was most surely coming.

Instead, Moon said, "It's okay, Svetlana. I'm not going to hurt you. I need you to answer a few questions, and I promise I'll be on my way."

Svetlana shouted, "Dmitri made me do it. It wasn't my idea. That son of a bitch never even gave me any money. He said I owed him for all the times I shortchanged him. He's a pig. Please don't hurt me. Let me go, and you can have me at no charge."

"I told you I'm not going to hurt you, okay? So calm down and give me some information, then you can return to business."

She took a deep breath and realized she might not get the shit beat out of her.

"I just want to know where Dimitri is and if he has that piece on him," Moon said.

"If I tell you, what happens to me? If he finds out, he'll kill me," Svetlana said.

"If you let me, I can help you. I know that wasn't your idea. But I'm a bad man, too, you should know."

Svetlana saw Moon's knife come out of his jacket. When Moon spoke next, it was quietly and slowly, "Where is he?"

"Roman's. A bar on Florida Ave."

"Does he have a gun?"

Svetlana's breathing slowed a bit. "Dmitri always has a gun and knife."

"Give me your heroin now! I know you're carrying, so don't lie to me. Hand it over."

Recalling the times she had been dope sick, Svetlana said, "Please don't take my stash. You'll make me sick if you take it."

"So then get sick."

From a collection of condoms, lipstick, and twenty-dollar bills in her jacket, she produced three small bundles of brown heroin.

Moon placed the heroin in his jacket. As he walked away, he said, "I'll get Dmitri out of your life. And then it'll be up to you to figure out where your life goes from here."

Even as he said it, though, he feared Svetlana was too far gone already. She remained glued to the lamppost until a car slowed down and the driver lowered his window. In the same way she had said a thousand times before, Svetlana chanted, "Hey, baby, are you looking for a date?"

16

MOON'S REVENGE

oman's bar was a box-like building with large plate-glass windows. Folding grates stood ready to secure the glass at closing time. The few remaining patrons filed out of the bar at almost two o'clock in the morning.

Moon spotted Dmitri as he staggered out and headed toward an older model Cadillac Seville. Dimitri looked like a drunken Russian bear swaying back and forth as he searched for his car. Moon was grateful he was three sheets to the wind; it would make overcoming him easier.

As Dmitri fumbled with his keys, Moon came up from behind, raised the blackjack over his head and brought it down four times on the big man's dome. The blows caused Dimitri to drop to the ground and pass out. Moon scooped up his keys, opened the back door, and crammed Dmitri into the back seat. Dimitri was relieved of his gun and knife, and Moon jumped into the front seat and started the Cadillac.

Moon drove down Florida Ave. toward the center of the city. He was looking for a particular building, and just before the intersection of Rhode Island Ave., he spotted it—a small branch office of the U.S. Postal Service.

Moon parked in front of the post office. He jumped out of the car and opened the back door. As a comatose Dimitri snorted and twitched, Moon poured the vodka on his clothes and down his mouth. Moon returned Dimitri's knife to his pocket and his gun to his waistband. Svetlana's heroin was shoved down the front of Dmitri's pants with full force and conviction.

Moon opened the trunk of the car and found the crowbar. Freeing the fury he felt for Dimitri he smashed the large front window of the post office. As the glass shattered and fell to the ground, the alarm sounded.

Moon pulled Dmitri out of the car and dragged him over to the window and rolled him into the building. Moon jumped over the counter, scooped up a fist full of stamps and put them in Dmitri's top pocket. The stamps were to add insult to injury, Moon thought there must be some federal law just for stealing stamps.

Moon walked back to the Caddy casually as police sirens signaled their approach. The Post Office is a federal building, so Moon brought him there because any crime committed in or around it is a federal crime. In that case, the FBI would need to investigate and charge the Russian. If convicted of breaking into a federal building, possessing firearms, heroin, and U.S. postage, he faced heavy time in federal jail and perhaps deportation. Moon doubted he was in the country legally.

Moon drove Dimitri's car back to his apartment and fought the adrenaline that was keeping him awake by pulling a bottle of Amaretto from under the sink and pouring himself a couple of shots. Sleep finally placed its veil over him around 5:00 a.m. Moon's last thoughts were of his plan to return to Rhode Island.

The first step would be to clean out his apartment and buy one of those fancy new flip phones, the untraceable kind. Then steal a set of plates for the Caddy and head north on Route 95. Returning to the mob after being a government informant was uncharted territory, but Moon knew it was his only option. He was hoping for a chance at redemption and a chance to start over. He was determined to do whatever it took to make this happen.

17

GINO'S DAY AT THE HOPE VALLEY BARRACKS
Winter 1989

Renée whispered, "Good morning, sweetie. You probably don't remember since you're a man, but today marks two years since we began dating."

Gino stumbled a bit. "Of course, I remember . . ."

"That's enough, it's not a test. This is my anniversary gift for you. I made you your favorite breakfast, three eggs scrambled, home fries, and a cinnamon raisin bagel with cream cheese."

"Thank you, babe. I'm sorry I didn't get you anything."

She gave him an alluring look and said, "I am sure you will be able to think of something when you get home."

A grinning Gino nodded and dove into his breakfast.

At 7:45 a.m., Gino pulled into the Hope Valley Barracks driveway and parked in the back. He was scheduled to take over the night shift at 8:00 a.m.

The barracks was located on Nooseneck Hill Road, which ran parallel to Interstate 95. Four garage stalls, two on each side of the building, were attached to the barracks and connected to the building. The garages were used for storage because the cruisers of the eighties and nineties were too wide to fit into a stall built for the cruisers of 1931.

Troopers of the Hope Valley patrol handled the towns of West Greenwich, Exeter, Hopkinton, Richmond, Charlestown, and Westerly. Among the seven patrol areas of the state police, it was the largest geographically.

Most of the town police departments were relatively small. In addition to investigating crimes, troopers responded to traffic accidents and enforced motor vehicle laws. Two detectives were assigned to the barracks to investigate any felony that was reported.

Most troopers, including Gino, longed for the action that was taking place on Interstate Route 95. As troopers patrolled the highway, they looked for drug mules, guns, and stolen vehicles.

Gino parked his cruiser in the parking lot and walked through the back door and into the dispatch area. The furniture was worn and archaic, the walls painted a drab dark green, and the floor was layered with the same tile that was installed in 1931.

Despite being almost sixty years old, the barracks glistened from the work of the troopers who cleaned, polished, and washed every inch. Before the day shift arrived, the trooper assigned to the overnight desk handled polishing the brass door handles, polishing the furniture, and waxing and buffing the floors.

Seated at the console this morning was Gino's academy classmate, Steve Gnight. While Gino approached Steve, he could see his eyelids becoming a battleground of opening and closing as the morning sun streamed through the windows.

"Hey seventeen," Gino said, calling Gnight by his badge number. The tension in Gnight's neck snapped back as he tightened his tie and wiped the grit from his chin and eyes.

"Good morning, twenty-eight, and good night for me. It's all yours," Gnight replied.

"Any prisoners locked up?" Gino said.

If there were, Gino would have to arrange to get them photographed and fingerprinted and then sent down to court in Westerly for arraignment.

"Nope, quiet night except for the circus truck that broke down and the elephants that escaped," replied Gnight. "No arrests were made after we corralled them."

Although Gino laughed, it wasn't funny at all, but what can you expect from a guy who had been awake for twenty-four hours? It was not his "A" material.

Gnight cleaned up the papers on the desk and typed on the day sheet, which was above the dispatch console, listing the day's activities. At 8:00 a.m., Trp. Gnight was relieved by Trp. Peterson, who was assigned to desk duty.

Taking off his uniform blouse, Gino hung it on the chair behind the console. With care, he slid his firearm into its holster and strapped it to his belt. For the next four hours, he sent his fellow troopers to investigate housebreaks, vandalism, larcenies, and accidents.

He would, among other things, obtain registration information, perform computer checks to determine whether someone had outstanding warrants, and gather any other information his brethren on the road needed.

Gino was eagerly awaiting his noontime relief to get out on the road at twelve-thirty. Gino dared not ask Cpl. Jim Doherty if he was relieved when he sauntered into the barracks.

When corporals asked a trooper a question, the trooper normally replied, "Yes, Corporal" or "No, Corporal." It is unthinkable that you would ever talk to a sergeant, and you probably would not even see a lieutenant. In most troopers' minds, the lieutenant looked down from heaven and only came down when you messed up.

"I'm ready to take over the desk, Peterson. Just give me a minute to take my blouse off."

Gino put on his blouse, adjusted his leather, and gave his boots a quick wipe with a rag from the bottom of the dispatch desk.

Jim Doherty returned with a lunch pail and a can of soda, which he placed on the console desk with the same care that he placed his butt onto the chair.

"All set, Peterson, go out there and make me proud," Doherty said with a wide grin.

"Yes, Corporal," Gino replied and hurried to his cruiser.

18

GINO PATROLS THE INTERSTATE

*I*t was two o'clock in the afternoon and Gino found an excellent place to see traffic on Route 95 north and south. Near the Connecticut-Rhode Island border, he eased the cruiser onto a grassy knoll halfway between Exits 1 and 2.

He was driving in his car, listening to the latest hit by The Young Rascals on his AM/FM radio, while he heard troopers answer calls and stop cars across the state via his police radio.

Gino's goal was more than just catching criminals. He also wanted to make his mother proud, not that he would ever admit that to Renée. By now, Renée understood how tight Gino and his mother had become since his father's death. But it had started even before then.

As a young kid pedaling his bike around the neighborhood, Gino didn't know better when a bookie asked him to take a package every Tuesday up to a grocery store and drop it off. For his efforts, Gino would be given twenty dollars. He did it several times, then went out and bought baseball cards with the money. Gino's mother said, "Where are you getting the money for all this?" Gino told her the truth, and his mother was determined to put a stop to that right then and there.

The only problem was letting the bookie know that he was no longer going to work for him.

Teresa asked, "So who is this bookie you're working for?"

"They call him Moon," he answered.

Teresa knew Moon from the neighborhood, and she would have no problem confronting him herself, but she knew that Gino would have more problems if his "mommy" was solving his problems.

"Gino, you go tell Mr. Capelli that you can no longer help him, understand?"

"Yes, but . . ."

"No buts. Just do what I told you to do," Teresa said sternly.

On Tuesday morning Gino peddled his J.C. Higgins bike to Atwells Ave. and met Moon. When he rolled up, he felt anxious, but as he got off his bike, he felt strangely calm.

Moon wore a velvet jogging suit with gold chains that exposed his hairy chest. "Hey kid, are you ready to make this week's delivery?"

"I'm sorry, Mr. Moon, but I can't deliver your packages for you anymore."

"Oh, little man, is that your mother talking?" Moon asked.

Gino didn't realize it, but he was about to make a choice that would define the rest of his life. He looked down at his sneakers and held out his hand, "I'm sorry, Mr. Moon, but I'm done. No hard feelings."

Moon was both stunned and impressed. This kid's got some balls, he thought to himself. "Okay, kid, I'll just find someone else. Now get the hell out of here."

Little did they know this was only the beginning of the intertwining of their lives.

 ▪   ▪   ▪

It was from his mother that Gino learned there was more than one way he could go: toward a good job and maybe a nice family and home of his own, or go to prison, or die on the streets, or become addicted to drugs. The life you chose would make you who you would become. The culture of the state police had now embedded integrity within Gino's bones.

Gino waited for a car to speed past while resting the portable radar gun between his legs. As he pointed the device at a vehicle, it showed the speed in flashing red lights.

A constant hum showed that the radar was ready to answer the age-old question: "Can you tell me how fast I was going?"

On Route 95, the speed limit was 55 mph, but Gino set the gun to flash when a vehicle exceeded 70 mph. After that, Gino would leave the nest and go hunting. He would never interfere with the legal search-and-seizure rules, but he could sometimes use them to his advantage to keep the highways clean.

When troopers suspected drugs, guns, or contraband might be involved, speed could be a convenient excuse to stop a vehicle.

To decide whether to stop a speeding vehicle, Gino considered many factors. He looked for license plates from New York and New Jersey and for a single driver in a late-model car traveling northbound on the highway.

The driver's "look" overshadowed all of this. Every cop could see the guilty look on their faces immediately, as if they had it written across their foreheads. Besides the look, it was also the shifty head, the vice-like hold on the wheel, and the almost overabundance of attention to the road.

Imagine a sixteen-year-old taking a driving lesson with an instructor, and that is how they all looked while driving down the highway smuggling drugs, stolen goods, and cars.

It was the ability to interpret "looks" which led to traffic stops and arrests. People who were speeding were praying you wouldn't pull them over. Their look was more mischievous than sinister.

Criminals traveling the highway with contraband had a distinct look. It was more like the look you have when you try to lie or are extremely nervous. That look would invariably lead to a traffic stop. The inability to look someone in the eye, nervous tics, and tugging at clothing were all warning signs. Only a pathological liar who has committed a lifetime of crimes could mask the look.

Gino watched traffic pass as an Oldsmobile Cutlass with New Jersey registration plates sped by, heading north. Gino pointed the radar gun at the car and pulled the trigger, getting a reading of seventy-one miles per hour. It was a driver wearing sunglasses and a ball cap. He couldn't see his eyes, but the speeding was enough to check him out.

As Gino emerged from the culvert, he turned on the overhead lights and pursued the Cutlass. Just north of Exit 2, he caught up with the car and made the stop. In case the driver came out shooting, he carefully angled the cruiser so that the front bumper pointed toward the highway. From behind his cruiser, he approached the car from the passenger's side. While doing this, the driver struggled to get his registration out of the glove box.

Gino knocked on the window with his right hand, keeping his left hand on his gun in case this traffic stop went wrong. With a nod, the driver acknowledged Gino and opened the window.

"License and registration, sir. The reason I stopped you was that you were traveling seventy-one miles per hour in a fifty-five-mile-per-hour hour zone."

Taking a guess at the driver's age, Gino figured he was in his midtwenties. Two diamond earrings added a sparkle to his dark complexion. As Gino asked him to remove the hat and sunglasses, he peered into dark brown eyes that reminded him of two cups of coffee.

While handing over his license and registration, he apologized, saying he was on his way to an interview at URI. Alonzo Garcia, a twenty-four-year-old from Sea Girt, New Jersey, gave Gino a letter from the University of Rhode Island informing him of an interview for a student affairs position at four o'clock.

Gino examined all the documents and said, "Just wait here for one minute, Mr. Garcia. I'll be right back."

As Gino returned to the cruiser, he radioed Cpl. Doherty all the information about Alonzo Garcia. The response was that his license and registration were active, and there were no warrants. After filling out the warning form, he returned to his car.

"Mr. Garcia, I am going to give you a warning for speeding. Please slow down, and I wish you good luck with your interview," Gino said.

After being slightly shocked, Alonzo Garcia thanked Gino and asked if he could go, and after receiving the nod from Gino pulled carefully out of the breakdown lane, hoping the warning was a good omen.

Gino filed the written warning with his other paperwork, including copies of speeding summonses and equipment violations. Troopers also filled out a form called a Field Intelligence Report when stopping known felons or members of organized crime.

Every road trooper had to account for every minute they spent on the road, so documenting this and every stop was important. Gino had to submit weekly activity reports listing arrests, citations, equipment violations, and field intelligence reports. It certainly wasn't the same as working for the Intelligence Unit, but sometimes he could convince himself he was doing some good after all.

Other calls he handled, like the domestics that didn't lead to an arrest, the missing person found after a quick search, lost dogs, neighborhood disputes, and the general insanity of humanity, made it into separate reports. One of Gino's sergeants was fond of saying, "We're what God sends you when your life goes to hell."

Supervisors expected you to handle all of that, and God forbid you didn't produce the activity they expected. There was no way a corporal was going to take any heat from a sergeant for a shift that didn't produce, and no sergeant was going to lose a part of his ass to a lieutenant who wasn't happy.

Shit flows downhill, and the troopers on the road are as downhill as it gets.

As Alonzo Garcia pulled away, Gino was about to pull into traffic himself when a passenger van flew past him like a bottle rocket. After fumbling for the radar gun, he locked the signal on the car and got a reading of 86 mph.

The wind of the engine sounded like a jet about to take off as he quickly pulled out and pushed his Plymouth Fury for all it was worth. After about ten minutes, he stopped the car just south of Exit 3, Route 138.

With his cruiser, angled as before, Gino approached the female operator.

"License and registration, please, ma'am. The reason I stopped you was that you were traveling at eighty-six miles an hour in a fifty-five-mile-an-hour zone."

During his time on the road, Gino heard many excuses from speeders. He was amazed by the number of people who were rushing to the hospital because a loved one was in serious condition, the number of doctors, nurses, etc. rushing to the hospital, lawyers late for court, and volunteer firefighters rushing to the fire station.

He'd heard them all, and typically the threat of the dispatch trooper calling to verify the story results in an apology and a slightly less urgent reason for speeding. Yet Gino was about to hear something he had never heard before. On approaching, he noticed a well-dressed, perfectly coiffured, middle-aged woman in the driver's seat. Keeping her hands on her steering wheel, she gripped it tightly as if letting go would send her spiraling downward.

She rolled down her window and looked directly into Gino's eyes. "Trooper, if I don't go to the bathroom soon, I'm going to shit my pants right here in my car. Feel free to follow me to the nearest bathroom, and you can give me a ticket, but I must leave now. Despite my PhD in English Literature and three kids, I haven't gone in my pants since I was a baby, and I don't plan to today."

Looking into her eyes, Gino could see that this was not bullshit, and even if it was, he wasn't willing to take the chance of dealing with the consequences.

"Please proceed to the next exit. Bear to the right, and you will see a gas station with a restroom." In response, she shifted into gear frantically, and her van hummed as it sped up. Gino didn't follow her because he had looked into many pairs of eyes in his lifetime . . . and knew those eyes weren't lying.

19

GINO SELECTS HIS PREY

It was almost four o'clock, and the winter sun was setting in the western sky; its work for the day was done. It would return tomorrow to repeat its responsibility to sustain one of its children, planet Earth.

Gino knew that with darkness came less traffic and more difficulty hunting his prey. He set up in the breakdown lane just north of Route 138. The four-leaf clover was closest to the Hope Valley Barracks. Those exiting westbound onto Route 138 and then Route 1 were headed toward URI, South County's beaches, and Newport.

The Post Road along the southern coast of Rhode Island, constructed in 1790, was now known as Route 1. After traveling south to Westerly, it entered Connecticut. Eventually, as the new nation grew, the route ended in Key West, Florida.

As the sky dimmed, a lone driver crossed from Connecticut into Rhode Island at exactly 55 mph. Ralph Carlini, or Ralphie as his friends called him, was feeling pretty good about himself, driving the exact speed limit.

Ralphie was a wannabe with the New Jersey organized crime, a small-time drug dealer who wanted to hit the big time. Today he was going to prove himself to the mob. As an associate, he believed he had earned enough respect to become a made man, a soldier in the Mafia. Hopefully, someday a capo who oversees his own crew. He was determined to show that he was a man of loyalty and courage. After all, those qualities would turn him into a respected and feared member of organized crime. He just had to prove it.

Ralphie had been a drug dealer ever since he dropped out of Riverdale Valley High School in Bayonne, New Jersey. He started selling weed to the kids in school and soon graduated to college students and yuppies.

Now at age twenty-five, Ralphie had a lucrative marijuana, cocaine, and heroin business that he ran with his cousin, "Little John" Menotti, who had connections with the New Jersey family.

Little John was fond of saying the only way to survive this criminal enterprise was to ensure the bosses got a piece of the action.

Ralphie learned that although the mob would disavow drug dealing, they always had a handout when it came to money and really didn't give a fuck where the money came from as long as they got a piece of the action.

Little John was the brain and brawn of the operation, and Ralphie oversaw marketing. Over many years, Ralphie had set up a reliable network of people that trusted him and that he trusted.

Trust is only extended to the last deal completed, with the possibility that the next deal could be a rip-off, or worse, a set-up. Ralphie didn't worry himself over such matters because he was high most of the time and never followed Little John's rule that you don't use your own product.

During the last nine years, they had made hundreds of thousands of dollars, most of which Ralphie spent on cocaine, marijuana, and snorting heroin. He spent money in cool nightclubs in Jersey filled with women who were treated to bottles of Dom Pérignon. Ralphie was also known to be generous with his wealth, often paying for his friends to join him on outings.

The only thing, in fact, that was more important than his lifestyle was greed—an addiction stronger than women, booze, and drugs. A mutual friend had introduced him to a man named El Hefè, who provided him and Little John with a variety of illegal substances.

Ralphie always paid the asking price without question. In this business, inquisitive minds ended up dead. He didn't care about the details of El Hefè's operation. All he cared about was getting what he wanted quickly and without any hassle. He knew that El Hefè was reliable and always had the best quality product. Ralphie knew that if he asked about El Hefe's operation, the consequences would be dire.

It was El Hefè who brought Ralphie and Little John the deal that would force the NJ mob to take notice. El Hefè had ten kilos of cocaine he had to get from Jersey to Providence and he didn't have any mules that he trusted with that quantity. El Hefè agreed to Ralphie's deal. The flow of drugs was constant and ever moving like a river, and at the end was the insatiable consumer. Like the Mississippi, no man could stop it.

Ralphie would transport the ten kilograms for ten thousand dollars. Four to six times their wholesale value would then be realized after the powder was cut (diluted), and repackaged into smaller, individual packets. The packets were then sold on the streets for double their wholesale value.

20

THE MULE

The ten kilos were carefully wrapped in plastic, then with another layer of plastic filled with coffee grounds to hide the smell from drug dogs.

A remote-controlled compartment was welded under the driver's seat. The carpet was carefully removed and then replaced. The emergency brake pedal was the switch to open the compartment.

When El Hefè looked at Ralphie, one of his eyes moved as he talked, but the right one continued to look to the right. While speaking, Ralphie wasn't sure which eye to look at, so he concentrated on his nose to avoid offending.

In sweatpants and tasseled loafers, El Hefè wore one of those light cotton shirts from South America. Short and rugged, he had an inviting face. His dark eyes sparkled with kindness and mischief. He had a gentle but determined air about him, as if he had seen a lot but still held onto his optimism. He smiled easily, and it was impossible not to smile back.

"Ralphie, listen to me, my young Italian friend. This is all you must do, and we both make a lot of money. It's just a four-hour car ride for you, and you make ten grand. What's wrong with that, my friend?" He laughed loudly.

Ralphie noticed the .357 in his waistband but didn't think much of it. He assumed there was much cocaine in the building and that El Hefè was responsible for it, so there was no doubt he would protect it with his life.

"What do I do when I get to Providence?" Ralphie asked.

"You go to the train station near the State House . . . now just shut up and listen."

"Okay, all right. Don't get nervous. When am I going to get my money?" Ralphie asked.

By asking about the money, El Hefè knew Ralphie was all in, and it was now time to tell him the rest of the plan.

"There's an extra thousand dollars in here for you, but you have to do something extra to get it. You must pick up another five kilograms from a friend before delivering our package. So rather than sending fifteen kilograms in one delivery, I am sending another associate with five kilograms on the train from NYC to Providence.

"This friend has been given an address, so you should pick him up from the train station and drive him there. When you arrive, deliver the packages, and go back to the train station. Leave him there and drive back to Jersey."

"Wait, that wasn't part of the deal," Ralphie protested. "How am I supposed to know who this guy is, and how am I supposed to trust him?"

As he fingered the gun in his waistband, El Hefè spoke slowly. "As soon as you get to the station, you wait outside in your car. Our friend will be carrying an Adidas sports bag and wearing a Yankees cap. Then, you drive him to the address I have given him. He's Italian, so you should be able to get along with him easily. You won't have to deal with him again once you get home. Of course, unless you like the easy money and wish to make more deliveries for me."

"Then I deliver and make ten grand for what I mule, plus another grand for bringing the mystery man to the address. Easy peasy."

"I think that's it. Get in your car and get out of here," El Hefè said.

21

GINO SNARES HIS PREY

Just north of Route 138, Gino pulled off the highway after his last traffic stop. Swinging the car around to face traffic perpendicularly, he wanted to see each car's passenger side directly as it sped northward.

Gino wondered what stories each driver would share if asked. Was it a salesman heading to his next stop, or a family heading to Boston for a reunion? Perhaps a husband and wife returning from visiting grandchildren in the Carolinas.

Thousands of lives, countless stories, going about their business and hoping that their lives wouldn't be altered by a car accident or a traffic ticket. Death, injury, and misfortune changed lives in an instant.

Seeing a 1987 Mercury Marquis barrel past him, Gino peered into its driver's window. The driver looked over and locked eyes with Gino for too long. The car almost drifted out of the lane because he was fixated on the state police cruiser.

Hallelujah, there was the look. Gino picked up his radar gun and pulled the trigger. Sixty-seven. Good enough. He put the car in gear, turned onto the highway, and headed after the Mercury. Gino took his time catching up with the vehicle and didn't activate his lights.

He wanted to see how the operator reacted to him pulling out. As he approached the car, he saw the operator looking in his rearview mirror and moving around like a nervous cat.

Gino radioed dispatch that he was stopping a tan Mercury Marquis, New Jersey, registration 987-J45, for a speeding violation on 95 just north of 138. He allowed the driver to continue driving for about a mile before hitting the lights and pulling the car over.

Ralphie lowered the window in the hope that the smell of smoked marijuana would be sucked out of the car. I have to play it cool, and I'll be fine. There's no way this pig is going to find my stash. No one catches Ralphie. If he gives me a ticket, I'll rip it up when he pulls away.

He noticed the Mountie hat and boots approaching, but he lost sight of him until he heard a knock at the passenger's window. He lowered the window and tried to play it cool.

"License and registration, sir. The reason I stopped you is that you were clocked on radar doing sixty-seven in a fifty-five-mile-per-hour zone," Gino said.

"Sure, Officer. Oh sorry, Trooper, just a second." Ralphie took his license from his wallet, opened the glove box, and took out the registration. He handed both to Gino.

When Gino leaned in to grab Ralphie's documents, a strong aroma of marijuana hit him in the face. He thought that if he inhaled deeply for a minute or two, he would be high as the operator.

"Is that marijuana I smell, sir?" Gino asked.

"I don't think so, Trooper, I mean, I borrowed this car from my friend, and who the fuck, oh sorry, who knows what he did before he gave it to me?" I am still cool as a cucumber, Ralphie thought.

"Sir, shut off the car and keep your hands on the steering wheel."

"Yes, sir," the cool one answered.

Gino stood on the side of the highway, he glanced at the documents while keeping an eye on the operator. According to the license, Ralph Carlini was born on March 1, 1965, and lived at 1865 River Ave. Apt. #3, Bayonne, New Jersey. Gino was intrigued by the registration, as it listed The American Leasing Company as the owner.

Mules were notorious for leasing cars to deliver their drugs. A mule would rent a car from a car dealer with a fake ID. They would always pay in cash, so tracking down the actual renter can be challenging.

Police officers had to take the suspect into custody and notify the rental company. As a result, the company had the authority to repossess the vehicle, eliminating the possibility of seizing it as a result of the criminal enterprise.

Gino decided to search the car because all the signs were there. The issue would be the legal cause for searching the car.

"Mr. Carlini, do you have any marijuana in this car?" Gino posed the first in a series of questions that would hopefully lead to the pot of gold at the rainbow's end.

"Oh no, sir. I don't do drugs," Ralphie responded.

"Well, there's a strong scent of marijuana coming out of the car, and I understand it might have been your friend's doing, but I'm sure you understand why I have to ask."

"Of course, sir, I understand you're just doing your job."

"And what do you do for a living, Mr. Carlini?"

In his shirt, Ralphie felt just a few beads of sweat leaving his armpits. "I'm sort of between jobs right now, but mostly I work in construction," Ralphie said.

Gino looked at this short guy, maybe five feet five at most, as thin as a stick figure. He looked more like a meth addict than a construction worker.

"Show me your hands," Gino said. Ralphie took his hands off the steering wheel, revealing hands that hadn't done a hard day's work in a lifetime. He probably never lifted anything heavier than an ounce of grass.

"Mr. Carlini, where are you headed?"

"I'm going to Boston to see a friend, you know, maybe catch a Bruins game. I hear the Devils are in town," Ralphie said.

"Okay, what's your friend's name and address?" Gino continued the inquisition.

Baseball was Gino's favorite sport, and he didn't follow hockey much. Renée, on the other hand, went to law school in Boston and loved hockey. Many nights Gino was forced to watch her beloved Bruins. Renée always insisted on staying up for the postgame show, so he knew the Bruins were on a West Coast swing.

"Ah, Vince Richards. I don't know exactly where he lives, but I'm supposed to call him when I get there."

"Mr. Carlini, you're not carrying any guns, narcotics, or anything like that, are you?"

"Oh no, sir, I would never do that."

Here it is. Wait for it, wait for it.

"Then you wouldn't mind if I searched your car? It would just take a minute, and then you can be on your way," Gino asked.

Gino got an incredible answer. "Yes, of course."

Ralphie didn't know why he said yes. What else could he say? His only hope was that this cop wouldn't discover the hide.

If Ralphie had said no, Gino would have had to get a search warrant for the car. He had no idea why they weren't schooled better, but that wasn't his problem. All he had on Ralphie was the smell of marijuana and the fact that he was speeding. A judge would not sign a warrant based on those facts.

"OK, sir, before I check your car, I have a form. It's a consent-to-search form. It says you understand your rights and consent to me searching your car," Gino asked nonchalantly.

"OK, sure," Ralphie said.

Gino filled out the form and had Ralphie initial each section, and then sign it at the bottom. He then told him to sit tight, and he would be right back to conduct the search. Gino radioed dispatch to request backup and let them know he was about to conduct a search.

He then asked Ralphie to step out of the car and put his hands on the trunk while he quickly searched the car. Ralphie complied, not knowing that his car was about to be torn apart.

Gino started in the driver's compartment, looking under the seat and reaching up under the console. He then moved to the passenger side and opened the glove box where he found a small bag of marijuana. In the ashtray, he found four roaches, the remnants of Ralphie smoking weed on his ride to Boston.

Searching the rear compartment revealed nothing other than some empty candy wrappers and an empty French fry container from McDonald's.

He then asked Ralphie to move to the side of the vehicle and place his hands on the roof as he took his keys and opened the trunk. He found nothing except a jack, a spare tire, and two quarts of oil. Gino slammed the trunk down out of frustration, then asked Ralphie to return to the rear of the car and place his hands on the trunk.

Gino received a call on his portable that Trooper Steve Regan was about five minutes away. He was about to tell him that he was all set when he noticed something unusual. The emergency brake pedal was engaged and pressed up against the carpet of the floor.

Gino had stopped hundreds of cars in his career, and no one ever engaged the emergency brake pedal when they were stopped—never.

He jumped into the passenger's seat and pulled on the release latch for the brake pedal located just to the left of the steering wheel. Gino then pulled the lever toward him and expected to release the brake, but it sounded like the latches of a suitcase had opened. He looked in amazement as he heard the rug on the floor of the passenger's compartment bulge forward.

Gino now faced a dilemma. He knew he had found the hide, but from the "Oh shit" he heard from the rear of the car Ralphie knew it too. So, he moved quickly to the back of the car and used his right forearm to push Ralphie's head onto the trunk. He then used his left hand to grab Ralphie's wrist and bend it behind him.

After slapping Ralphie with cuffs, he pulled up on the links between his cuffs. This caused Ralphie's face to fall back onto the trunk. After Gino read him his rights, Ralphie remained silent despite Gino's repeated questioning.

As they waited for Trp. Regan, there was an awkward silence between them. Cars with curious onlookers passed by and gazed at the show. Gino paid no attention; his primary focus was securing Ralphie until help arrived.

So, it was no surprise he overlooked the Cadillac Seville, bearing Virginia plates, pass by at fifty-five miles per hour, its operator humming to the dulcet tones of Frank Sinatra singing "The Summer Wind."

A RI State Trooper's uniform caught Moon Capelli's attention as he passed by. He also saw the trooper holding a short man's head down on the trunk. It seems that not much has changed since I left, Moon thought.

Trp. Steven Regan arrived on the scene. "Looks like he pissed himself. There's got to be something going on here," Regan told Gino. The two wrapped a throwaway paper blanket around Ralphie's waist and secured him in Gino's cruiser.

Regan watched Gino carefully cut around the carpet with his Swiss Army knife. When he pulled the carpet away, he peered into a compartment containing ten neatly packaged kilos of cocaine. When they got it back to the barracks, they would field-test it, but he knew he had struck gold from the look on Ralphie's face.

22

COOPERATION OBTAINED THE HARD WAY

Gino drove Ralphie back to the barracks with Regan close behind. At the barracks, he was given a paper suit to wear, and his soiled pants were discarded.

The ten packages were laid out on a large table in the barracks conference room. Unlike movies and television shows where cops test the substance by putting it on their tongues, Regan opened one with a pen knife. He scooped a small portion of the white powder into the test kit. It was a small plastic container with an ampoule of white liquid inside.

Once the powder was placed in the container, Regan pressed the ampoule until it broke. When the liquid touched the powder, a bright blue color appeared, as vivid as pictures of the Earth's oceans taken from a NASA satellite. The bluer the mixture, the purer the coke, and this batch was pure.

Ralphie was taken out of his cell and marched to the same conference room. The product that would propel him into the mob was safely locked away in the evidence room.

Gino read Ralphie his rights again with Regan as his witness.

Ralphie said, "I know my rights, and by the way, you're an asshole."

Gino snapped back, "I'm an asshole? You're the one smuggling that poison."

"It's not even my car; if there's stuff in there, it was planted."

Gino decided it was time to try a different tactic. When he was in the Intelligence Unit, he used a technique that involved explaining the suspect's situation and then helping by speaking with the prosecutor. Ralphie was approached in a similar manner by Gino. Gino proposed that Ralphie should help in exchange for prosecutor consideration.

Regan just sat back and let Gino take the lead. "You're going down, Carlini, for possession of ten keys. Why don't you make it easy on yourself and tell us who gave it to you and where you were taking it?"

"Go fuck yourself, pig. You got nothing on me. My lawyer will have this case dropped in a heartbeat," Ralphie said.

Wrong answer.

Gino also thought this could drag on for some time, the sparring back and forth, the matching of wits with the witless. Perhaps he and Regan could do the good cop, bad cop routine for a while, but sometimes you just hit a brick wall.

Gino was rethinking his approach when Regan suddenly got off his chair and lunged for Ralphie. He reached down between Ralphie's legs and grabbed the family jewels. He slowly increased the pressure in his hands, and just as slowly, Ralphie came out of his chair and peered up at Regan. Tears welled up in his eyes.

"Listen to me, Mr. Carlini," squeezing a bit tighter, "you are going to tell me where you got the drugs and where they are heading." Still tighter. "Do you understand me?"

Ralphie started to cry and begged for the release of Regan's grip; he feared he would never have any children if this was kept up.

"All right, all right. Listen to me. Please stop asking me who I got the drugs from. He's Columbian, and I'll be dead if I tell you. So please just arrest me, and I'll do the time. I'll give you the guy I was supposed to meet at the train station. He's carrying five keys, and he knows where the stuff is going to be delivered. So, look, you get fifteen keys out of this and maybe I do my time up here. And I stay alive."

23

TRAIN STATION ARREST

*L*ater that day, Gino wore a Beatles sweatshirt, jeans, and Nike sneakers. His snub nose .38 was strapped to his ankle, and his handcuffs were in his back pocket. He relished being out of uniform and back in plain clothes. Despite this short stint with the Narcotics Unit, Gino felt like a detective again.

Upon entering the train station, Gino wondered where the suspect might run to escape arrest. Where should he position himself? Growing up in Providence, he knew the surrounding area, which would have been in his favor if the suspect wasn't from the city.

The station was in the middle of Providence's financial district, just opposite the south lawn of Rhode Island's imposing State House where legislators made the laws that Gino enforced.

The Amtrak train station contrasted the magnificence of the State House. A block-long nondescript brick building with no windows, it was made of coarse cement, inside and out. Its transparent dome and large glass doors on both sides provided the only natural light. One opened onto Gaspee Street, and the other to a semicircular street used by cabbies and travelers picking up or dropping off riders. Nearly kissing wooden circular benches surrounded the room but were separated in two to allow travelers to sit and check out the giant tote board showing train arrival and departure times.

Today, there was a mix of people arriving and leaving: older adults looking to save money by taking the train instead of flying, college students, and families fleeing a harsh winter.

The two narcotics detectives paid little attention to Gino. He assumed they were saddled with him because he made a significant grab on the highway, and they knew about his history and romance with Michelle.

Detectives Richard Sullivan and Leon "Babe" Blanchette were veteran narcotics detectives well-versed in the Kabuki dance that was about to occur. Sullivan was about six feet tall with an average build. His brown hair was slicked back and fell on his shoulders.

He wore a jean jacket, polo shirt, and black jeans. A leather jacket hid his snub nose .357 Magnum, handcuffs, and extra ammunition delicately hanging under each arm courtesy of his shoulder holster.

"Babe" was short, about five feet nine, with a buzz cut left over from his stint in the Marine Corps. A permanent scowl on his face went along with the scar crossing the bridge of his nose as it headed toward his cheek. There were legions of stories about how he got the scar, but no one had the balls to ask him.

If you met Babe, you wouldn't ask either.

Strange as it may seem, Babe also happened to be the most proficient undercover detective in the department. He would often use his less-than-charming attitude to intimidate dealers into selling him drugs, posing as a soldier who got hooked on them when he was overseas.

Gino had gotten Ralphie to give up the mule that was supposed to arrive on the train from New York City. The mule knew he was being picked up on Gaspee Street outside the station, but he had no idea who would pick him up. According to Gino, the mule was wearing a Yankees baseball cap and carrying an Adidas sports bag holding five kilograms of coke.

Gino and the detectives took their positions at seven as the train arrived. Babe and Richard stood at the two exits, while Gino stood at the top of the escalator.

Passengers got off the train underground. As the travelers reached the top of the escalator on their way to the terminal, Gino scanned them quickly for hats and sports bags. The first people to reach the top of the escalator were a couple, who appeared to be in their twenties traveling with three kids.

Many freckles covered the woman's face, and her hair was short with red highlights. She was wearing orange pants, a blue shirt, and her feet were adorned with open-toed sandals.

She herded the three youngsters and their suitcases to the base of the escalator. Her husband helped the process along by giving each of his children a small bag and placing them on the electric stairs one at a time.

The youngest, about five years old, had his name on a handwritten note attached to the back of his shirt with a diaper pin. Gino watched backpacks, drink boxes, and bags of snacks as the family passed by, but no Adidas sports bag.

They were followed by two young girls in jeans, Brown University sweat shirts, and flip-flops. They were young and giddy and not interested in anything happening around them.

Then Gino spotted him. Hanging back toward the end of the line of escalator riders. He was wearing a Yankees cap turned to the side, a plain black T-shirt, and gray sweatpants with grease stains that led from one pocket down to the cuff.

He kept his head down and did his darndest to blend into the crowd, eyes darting around like a ping-pong ball. He was as inconspicuous as a white tiger on the African plain.

The mule looked more Italian than Gino did. He was short and muscular, wearing a wife-beater T-shirt, which exposed his hairy shoulders, biceps, and forearms. In fact, he had so much body hair it was difficult to see the Italian flag tattoo on his right bicep.

The brim of his cap could barely contain the abundance of untamed, black, curly locks that spilled out from beneath it. His prominent Roman nose and large ears were complemented by deep brown eyes, altogether creating a striking facial ensemble.

As the suspect reached the top of the escalator, Gino saw the blue sports bag with the white Adidas name and logo emblazoned across the front. After signaling to the two narcotics detectives that the target had been found, he followed him to the door leading onto Gaspee Street.

As the suspect exited the station, Sullivan approached him head-on with a smile, like someone about to ask for directions.

"Excuse me, sir, my name is Detective Richard Sullivan of the Rhode Island State Police. Can I ask you a few questions?"

"Ah, sure," the mule said as he stared at his badge. A sudden sense of reality struck the man, and he instinctively dropped the Adidas bag. Taking a step away from it, he looked around at the three detectives surrounding him. Running was out of the question. Several passengers turned their heads toward the commotion. Out of curiosity, they wondered what was going on.

"That's not mine!"

"What's your name, son?" Sullivan suddenly sounded like a guidance counselor.

"My name is Ronnie Ricci," he replied.

"Can I see some identification?" Sullivan asked. Ronnie produced a State of New York license with a Queens address.

"Mr. Ricci, do you mind if I look in your gym bag?"

Ronnie still wanted to run, but his legs felt like two cement blocks.

Ricci answered quickly as if the faster he talked the wider distance he could put between him and the bag. "It's not mine, sir. I don't care if you look in it."

"Okay," Sullivan said, "but we all just saw you drop it, so it's yours as far as we're concerned. I have to ask you for permission to take a look, and I guess you're all right with that. Can we look?"

Ricci squirmed a bit, tugged at his T-shirt, and grunted. He then nodded his head up and down with closed eyes. Babe picked up the sports bag, unzipped it, reached in, and pulled out one of the bag's five kilos. He quickly showed it to the mule and then shoved it back into the bag.

"You're under arrest," Sullivan said as Babe spun him around and cuffed him. He then led Ricci to the back wall of the train station. Babe kicked his ankles apart as far as his legs would allow and had him spread eagle against the building. The side of his face was practically embedded in the cold cement as Babe turned his head to the right.

They were surrounded by a small crowd when Sullivan pulled his badge and asked everyone to return to their seats. Sullivan then proceeded to ask the crowd to disperse. The people reluctantly complied, and Sullivan finally restored order to the situation.

Babe held him while Gino searched him and found two marijuana cigarettes and a package of Camels. He emptied out the cigarettes, and inside the pack was a rolled-up piece of paper. Gino unrolled it and read the address out loud.

"Three forty-seven Webster Avenue."

"Is that where you're supposed to deliver the coke?" Babe asked.

Ricci responded, although it was difficult to understand him because his cheeks and jaw were firmly against the cement wall. His words were garbled. "Look, you got me, but that's all you get. I'm not committing suicide. Like I said, that's not my bag, and I don't know what's in it or anything about that address. I found those cigarettes on the train."

Sullivan turned his attention to Gino. "Babe and I will take him to Hope Valley Barracks for processing. You take the dope and meet us there so we can do a field test. At some point, we will take a sample to the state crime lab for confirmation that it's cocaine."

They hustled Ricci into the cruiser parked in front of the State House, away from the station. Gino's car was parked in Kennedy Plaza, a short walk from the station. As he walked to his car, he wondered how many people would ever think he was carrying five kilos of cocaine.

24

GINO MAKES HIS CASE TO JOIN THE NARCOTICS UNIT

As Gino drove to the barracks, he recalled his conversation with Babe as they waited for the mule. He had asked Babe about his chances of getting into the Narcotics Unit after snagging ten kilos off the highway. Gino saw this as a potential opportunity to return to the Narcotics Unit, which could ultimately pave the way for his reentry into the Intelligence Unit.

There was no bullshit in this former Marine. The Corps and the state police were his only concerns, not hurt feelings.

Babe explained to Gino that narcotics work was different from investigating mobsters. The hours were long, the snitches were unreliable, and stopping the flow of drugs was like trying to hold back the tide.

"Look, Gino, even if you did join, you'd be at a disadvantage. Drug dealers will not trust anyone big and tall. That just screams cop to them. That's why everyone in the unit is relatively small compared to the rest of the department. I would also say that we have a different look. None of us look like the stereotypical detective. You can't just add some long hair or a beard or mustache and think you're a narcotics detective. It takes more than street clothes, my friend."

"Come on, Babe, you know I'm a hard worker. I can't believe I wouldn't fit in," Gino said.

"I know you're a hard worker, kid. But what's your end game?"

"It eats at me every day that I can't get back to Intelligence. I need to do something extraordinary to prove myself, and even then, I'm not sure if I can get the colonel's respect. I just need to find a way to show him that I'm capable of more than what I've been doing. It's my only hope." Gino was pleading and he hated himself.

"There is no doubt in my mind, Gino. This is not the place for you. Let me give you a few words of advice. When that fuck-up happened six years ago, you were like dog shit. Everyone avoided you; you stunk. Many avoided you because they didn't want dog shit on their shoes. But like dog shit, if you wait long enough, it dries up and blows away, and no one remembers.

"You're just at the point where people on the job are willing to forget. So, you might get another shot, but it won't be with us."

25

THE PRESS CONFERENCE

The Hope Valley Barracks were only a forty-minute drive from the train station. After exiting at Route 3 off Route 95, the barracks were just a short distance from the highway. The anticipation for the press conference increased as he got closer.

Gino knew exactly what would happen. Putting on a show for the press with the fifteen kilos would be the detectives' way of celebrating their victory in the war on drugs. He and the others understood that for every kilo they took off the highway, another thousand reached its destination.

My ass, Gino thought, *if this was a real war, we would have surrendered years ago.*

When he arrived at the barracks, his corporal greeted him and told him the detectives were setting up in the meeting room.

"Setting up for the press conference, Corporal?" Gino asked.

"Yup, you didn't think they would miss the chance to declare that they had defeated the menace of drug dealing, did you?" the corporal replied.

After Gino turned over the ten kilos from the car stop, fifteen kilos were laid out on blankets emblazoned with the RI State Police patch. In their pontificating, they proclaimed they had taken a significant amount of drugs off the streets.

Except for the dealer who lost all those drugs, no one would question them or give a damn.

Because the high-end dealers sold so much product, Gino knew they would lose nothing. If a midlevel dealer failed to deliver a load, however, then he would owe the money or his life.

For a split-second Gino thought this news conference would be a positive moment for him. Maybe the publicity would catch the attention of Colonel Walter E. Smith. He was known for ruling his troops with an iron fist. However, he also believed in second chances.

If you worked hard and showed him that you had learned from your mistakes, he would let you work your way back. Gino had seen many troopers who had screwed up, including his classmate who, in a drunken state, fired a few shots into the air on the lawn of his ex-wife's house. He ended up being suspended for six months. A year later, after several good arrests, he returned to detective work.

As the press entered the barracks, they set up their cameras and opened their notepads. Sullivan stood at an old podium and Babe was at the end of the table displaying the drugs and watching them with an eagle eye as serious as shit. A less-than-ideal male version of a stylish model at a car show in Detroit.

"Ladies and gentlemen," Sullivan began, "this morning, as the result of a traffic stop on Route 95 the state police were able to seize ten kilos of cocaine and arrest one individual. A subsequent investigation by detectives led to the seizure of an additional five kilos of cocaine at the train station in Providence."

As cameras whirled and reporters wrote furiously on their mini notepads, Sullivan continued. "Ralph Carlini of Bayonne, New Jersey, and Ronnie Ricci of New York City were arrested and charged with possession with intent to deliver.

"The arraignment is this afternoon in district court. The press release being distributed by Det. Blanchette has more information. As the investigation is ongoing, I cannot answer any questions. Thank you very much."

They were too busy doing the "perp walk" with Carlini and Ricci from the barracks to the car to answer reporters' questions on the spot, but they screamed them out anyway. Cameramen filmed the scene for broadcast later that evening.

As they positioned their prisoners in the back of the car, Gino approached Sullivan as he eased himself behind the steering wheel.

"Detective, what's next?"

"Secure the evidence at the barracks today. Tomorrow, bring it up to headquarters and log it into the evidence room, Trooper," Sullivan said before starting his car.

26

ANTICIPATION

enée was sitting on the couch reading some essay papers from her students when Gino got home around nine that night. She was wearing gray sweatpants and a Providence College sweatshirt. The sweatshirt had a deep cut starting at the front collar and plunging low enough to expose her chest. A pen was carefully positioned just behind her right ear, and glasses she'd never worn in public rested across the bridge of her nose.

She hardly noticed Gino walk through the door because she was engrossed in her papers and half listening to CNN's coverage of Saddam Hussein's invasion of Kuwait.

"Hey, professor."

"Sorry, I didn't hear you coming in. How was your day?" she asked.

Gino told her about the press conference and the impending trip to headquarters.

With some concern, Renée asked, "How do you expect that to go? Isn't it the first time you will have seen her since you were both transferred? At least as far as I know."

"C'mon Renée, that's not fair. You know I haven't seen her."

Backpedaling a bit, Renée said, "Sorry, just a little jealous, that's all."

"There's no reason for you to be jealous. It's going to be more of a confrontation, not a reunion," Gino said.

Renée noticed the storm clouds gathering across his face and changed the subject. He smiled and asked her about the weekend. She was relieved that the tension had been broken and they were able to enjoy the rest of their conversation without any awkwardness.

"I have some beef stew in the crockpot, and I stopped at the bakery and got some sourdough bread, so we can eat whenever you'd like," she said.

Gino poured two shot glasses of Celtic Crossing, a fine Irish whiskey, and sat next to her. As he gave her the whiskey, he said, "Cheers. Here's to your fine Irish posterior."

She laughed. "And here's to your thick Italian head."

27

CHAIN OF EVIDENCE

*T*his morning, Gino dressed slowly and deliberately. He left the apartment at precisely 7:00 a.m. while Renée was still sleeping. As soon as he picked up the fifteen kilos, he planned to travel to state police headquarters.

As was her habit, Gino knew Michelle would arrive early. He knew he had to deal with her, but he also hoped he might catch the eye of any brass who started showing up.

At seven-thirty in the morning, Gino walked into the Hope Valley Barracks and was greeted by a young trooper struggling to keep her eyes open. Gino walked behind the dispatch desk and grabbed the key to the converted closet that served as the evidence room. In the logbook, he entered his name and all the pertinent information for the sports bag and the fifteen kilos. Taking note of the daily log, the sleepy trooper signed the logbook.

7:30 a.m. Trp. Peterson logs out fifteen kilos of cocaine and one sports bag from evidence room Case 90-110, en route to HQ evidence room.

She sat back in her chair and resumed her battle with the sleep fairy.

Gino traveled north on Route 95 with his precious cargo by his side. From Route 95, he took Route 295 North until he reached Route 6 West. As he exited the highway, he traveled from Johnston into Scituate. With every mile, the scenery became increasingly rural. He passed through the quaint village of North Scituate with its stark white houses and small Catholic Church.

Gino drove through the village and crossed over the horseshoe-shaped dam that straddled the Scituate Reservoir, Providence's main drinking water supply. No less than a mile after passing the reservoir, the state police complex appeared to his right. The headquarters is the latest and most prominent building in the complex. Gino approached it. There is no doubt that this low-bidder state building was horrendously designed. A hollowed-out cinder block wall surrounded the entire building, giving it the appearance of a prison.

One of the most elite state police organizations in the nation was housed in a building with a flat roof that constantly leaked, rust-covered drainpipes, and a glass door with a stenciled state police logo.

The security codes for the back doors had been taken from him, so he entered through the front door and into the vestibule. Mrs. Ethel Lambert, a beloved member of the state police family, welcomed him. Her sweetness was only matched by her capability; she handled every phone call with dignity, regardless of the situation. The privacy of her troopers was paramount to her, and she kept secrets better than any priest.

The switchboard had ten incoming lines and fifty transfer buttons to route calls through headquarters and the six barracks covering the state. In a small cubicle near Mrs. Lambert's desk, a radio console was located.

Gino remembered the blizzard of 1978 when he was assigned to the radio. When Mrs. Lambert's shift was over, she stayed at the switchboard to help with the endless calls.

In February of that year, the state was buried in thirty-eight inches of snow that fell in a little over a day accompanied by seventy-mile-an-hour wind. As a result, many people were without electricity and hundreds were stranded on the highways. For those whose cars were stuck police stations, fire stations, and barracks became shelters.

Mrs. Lambert constantly fielded calls from frustrated people without power, elderly people worried about getting prescriptions, requests for rides from health-care workers, and a slew of others from the desperate and the impatient. Her approach alternated between grace-filled and stern when necessary.

Gino was sent to help her, and he dispatched troops on snowmobiles to deliver prescriptions and transport essential workers. Since cruisers could not move, the National Guard sent heavy-duty jeeps to each barracks.

All state troopers were called back to work. At the Scituate Barracks, troopers were divided equally between day and night shifts by the lieutenant. Twelve-hour shifts were scheduled for them. As they did when the state police were founded, Gino enjoyed sleeping in the barracks.

It was the first time he understood what his Uncle Earl had experienced as a trooper in the fifties and sixties. During the twenty-four hours the troopers spent together, a lot of activity occurred. They played an important role in restoring the state's ability to function. In between the serious moments, there were moments of humor.

"Trooper Peterson, I have a reporter from the *Providence Journal* on the line. Can you speak with him?"

"Sure, send it over."

Gino answered, "State Police Headquarters, Trooper Peterson speaking."

"Ross Darling here, Trooper; sorry to bother you, but what's the weather like?"

How's the weather? He wanted to say, "Look out the window, you dumb SOB," but Gino had another plan.

"Mr. Darling, it's eighty degrees and sunny. The men are on the roof working, sunning themselves."

The line went silent until Gino said, "Mr. Darling, Mr. Darling?"

"All set, Trooper. Sorry to bother you."

Gino laughed and went back to the chaos.

28

THE CONFRONTATION

"Hello, Trooper Peterson, it's been a long time," Mrs. Lambert said. About fifty years old, she had a mother's kind face and comforting smile. She wore a plaid wool skirt and a cashmere cardigan with her ever-present pen lodged behind her ear.

"Yes, Mrs. Lambert, it's been a while. I hope you're well?"

"I'm doing well. Thanks for asking," she replied.

Mrs. Lambert knew all about the Gino and Michelle problem. However, her question was vague. She would never ask directly; she didn't have to. Eventually, she found out everything. Because troopers sat next to her for the majority of the day, she would learn all about them. She knew their ambitions and their challenges, their insecurities, and their rivalries. Because she was well-known for not gossiping, she was always treated with respect.

"Oh, you know, Mrs. Lambert, I'm getting by," Gino said.

Then he quickly changed the subject. "I'm here to check in some evidence."

"I know," she said, "Sgt. Elbert told me to buzz you in when you get here. So, you go ahead, Trooper; I will let him know you're on the way to the evidence room. And Gino? Sometimes you have to pick your head up from the individual pieces of evidence to see the truth of a case."

Gino was sure Mrs. Lambert was trying to deliver a message, but she gave away nothing explicit. Instead, she simply pressed the small black button beside the telephone console. In this way, the lock on the door that separated the public from State Police Headquarters was released. Gino tugged on the black metal handle of the door after he heard the lock disengage. He tried not to draw attention to himself as he walked through the busy detectives' offices. He was in no mood to hear snide remarks about his fall from grace. Cops preyed on any chink in someone's armor, and for some of the detectives, an opportunity to jab at someone like Gino would not be passed up.

It was like sitting in an office full of traders at the New York Stock Exchange. They engaged in conversations through telephone calls, used vintage typewriters to document information, interacted with witnesses to collect testimony, and savored cups of coffee during their work. Division Desk Sergeant Bill Elbert managed the chaos. As Gino approached, Elbert held up a palm while talking on the phone.

He and Michelle were conversing. "Corporal Urban, Trooper Peterson is here with evidence from the Route 95 drug bust and the second arrest at the train station."

Elbert looked up from his desk and stared at Gino as he talked to Michelle. Gino averted his eyes and fiddled with the sports bag that he had placed on the edge of Elbert's desk.

Elbert grunted and pointed to the corridor leading to the evidence room. Gino headed to the rear of the building. In 1960, when the building was built, the room was probably more than adequately sized to hold seized evidence, but at this point, it was overcrowded with guns, rifles, drugs, clothing, and everything else imaginable recovered at a crime scene.

Walking into the room, he saw Michelle standing behind a wire mesh and sheet metal barrier. If you weren't depressed when you walked in, you were by the time you left. Michelle was confined to a room that looked like a yard sale on methamphetamines, and he could only imagine what she was living through.

She stood behind a half-metal, half-plastic French door with a large hole for conversation. Her back was turned slightly to the side as she arranged some evidence. She stood and walked to the door as he approached. Unlatching the top of the door, she swung it open without any sign of recognition or welcome.

Although she looked much the same as when he last saw her, seeing her in uniform was new to him. On her belt was a small handgun concealed in a holster. She wore uniform pants, a gray shirt, and a black military tie. The uniform showed off her petite frame.

When he approached Michelle, his knees ached. His body was flooded with adrenaline, which caused his heart to race and his palms to sweat. She was entering information into a huge evidence logbook. As always, her uniform was meticulously pressed, and her boots glistened in the fluorescent lights. Gino remembered her trim and athletic body despite her uniform hiding it.

Her blond hair was cut just as he remembered, stylish in its simplicity. However, it was long enough to put in a bun, and when she took it down, her hair rested comfortably on her neck and shoulders.

As she approached him, Michelle's crystal green eyes narrowed.

"Good morning, Michelle," he said. He hoped that his casual approach would be welcomed. Gino hated conflict, despite being a cop.

"Please refer to me as corporal," she replied.

"I'm here to check in fifteen kilos of cocaine, Corporal, from the Carlini and Ricci arrests." Michelle pushed some papers at Gino and took the fifteen kilos into the evidence room.

She worked in a small, insignificant office well below her intelligence and abilities. Even though she acknowledged it, her domain remained unchanged. He had to confront the reality of her world.

As soon as he had filled out the paperwork, he handed it to her. "Is there anything else you need from me? Corporal?" His question was dripping with sarcasm. It seemed to be the only weapon he had in this small battle.

Michelle came back at him sharply. "I beg your pardon, Trooper."

"Look, Michelle, I'm sorry you have to deal with me. I just wanted to log the evidence without any drama."

Suddenly, Michelle's voice changed to a low, gravelly growl. That tone of voice scared people the most; Gino was no exception. It's far easier to dismiss someone who screams and hollers, but a slow, deliberate speech pattern delivered in a low octave communicates dread for the listener.

"Drama? You didn't want any drama? Do you see me behind this counter?"

"But . . ." he tried to defend himself.

The more personal her words became, the more he looked around, hoping no one could hear, but she didn't seem to care.

She railed on. "It gets better, doesn't it, Gino. Not only do we get tossed out of the unit, but you end up living with another woman who swooped in when she saw an opening."

The chill had disappeared, and Gino felt his face become hotter. He tilted his chin up slightly, felt his heart pound and thought, *'Hell hath no fury,'* his anger simmering just beneath the surface.

"Wait a minute, that's my girl, and we got together after you and I separated," Gino realized, his heart racing.

They were so close now that they could feel each other's breath. Michelle was taking deep breaths, and as she exhaled, she steeled herself and spoke, the tension in the air palpable.

"We split up because you couldn't handle the shitshow, and you know exactly what she had to do with it. You didn't have the balls to weather the storm with me. You ran from me like the plague. We should have gone through that together."

Gino tried to catch his breath, hoping to recover. However, although he had played out this scenario a thousand times, nothing he had planned on saying came to mind. It never occurred to him how badly he had hurt her.

"Face it, Michelle, you and I will never live happily ever after. The colonel loved your dad, and you were his legacy. No one trusted me. What were our chances of making it?"

"You never even tried. You turned to pain pills. That's right, I know all about your love affair with Vicodin." She was holding nothing back.

"When I hurt my back lifting weights, I started taking them. That's the only reason I take them." Gino tried to defend himself, but she was right; just before he left for headquarters, he had taken two more. It was like he had lost the ability to cope without them.

Gino had fallen into the habit of taking one or two Vicodin a day. Each of the white pills contained 7.5 mg of hydrocodone and 500 mg of acetaminophen. Gino liked how it made him feel, not really high, but with a feeling that everything would be all right that day. If he felt a headache coming on, an upset stomach, or anxiety, everything faded away when the pills started working. With large white pills and prescription bottles, the road to addiction was paved.

Gino told himself: *I do not consider myself a junkie. Why not take a few pills my doctor prescribed? My habit doesn't require me to steal. My doctor was very accommodating about refills. He's a doctor. Shouldn't he know what he's doing?*

Still, he felt his heart race. Only Michelle's small circular fan whirred in the eerie silence.

"Are we finished, Corporal? I have to get back to the barracks."

"That's all, Trooper. You'll have to return to pick up evidence for the trial. Sgt. Elbert will let you know when we receive notice of the trial date. You know the drill," she calmed a bit, more professional but still speaking in a monotone.

He turned to leave, saying, "I get it, Corporal."

▪ ▪ ▪

Michelle knew she had pissed him off by talking about Renée, but she didn't care. He was the love of her life, and that bitch took him away.

She turned away from him and did not watch him go. She pushed down the longing she felt in her gut. In order to keep Gino at a distance, she assumed the icy demeanor of a queen, locking away her longing for him and burying her feelings deep within. In her mind, she repeated over and over: You are not getting to me! Gino, you're not!

But in many ways, he did get to her. His uniform still looked sharp as he walked away. He had the same dark brown eyes she remembered staring into many times. His hands were strong and rough. Finger veins were visible. From doing pushups at his cousin's Kenpo Karate Studio, his first two knuckles were large and unsightly. He had a strong jawline and a determined look in his eyes.

His presence was commanding, but his voice was gentle. He had an air of confidence and strength. All of it was still fresh in her mind, how those hands had held her, touched her cheek. His choice of another woman was like a punch to the gut.

29

MOON STARTS HIS JOURNEY
TO RHODE ISLAND
Winter 1989

As Moon Capelli drove toward Rhode Island, he realized he had been on the highway too long in a stolen car. The time had come for him to switch cars and find a new income source.

Leaving the highway, Moon headed for T.F. Green Airport in Warwick. It was late February, and darkness enveloped Moon's memories of the airport.

He had been forced to fly into Green a few times while in the service and making his way home. It was a place with lost luggage and terrible facilities, where you couldn't even find a bar that wasn't filled with pissed-off people. That didn't matter today. It would be the darkness that would protect him. The depression that gripped those who had to travel through this airport would work in his favor.

Leaving Dmitri's Cadillac in the long-term parking lot, Moon ditched the car that had served him so well; it would be months before the car was checked.

In the terminal, Moon looked at the departure and arrival boards for flights leaving for the West Coast or overseas. A Delta flight was scheduled to leave gate sixteen in fifteen minutes, with the eventual destination of San Diego. On his way to the gate, he stopped at a kiosk to buy some cheap luggage, then deliberately made his way to the check-in desk. Like a typical traveler, he was preoccupied and had his head down.

As Moon approached the passenger area, he noticed a group of travelers about to board their plane for California. Moon spotted his victim among the passengers. Approximately forty-five years of age, bald, neatly trimmed beard. There was a beak-like nose separating eyes that radiated confusion. A suit that was at least two sizes too small made him look uncomfortable. In addition to his boarding pass, he held a beeper and a coffee. In an attempt to silence the buzzing beeper, his thumb worked vigorously.

Moon used the opportunity to walk past him and bump him ever so slightly. After saying "excuse me," he gently lifted the man's wallet from his back pocket. With his head down, he walked away from the crowd and headed to the nearest men's room.

Hopefully, his victim would be over the Rocky Mountains before he realized his wallet was missing and then hope that he had left it at the ticket counter or packed it in his checked luggage. His flight would continue with him thinking that all would go well when he landed.

Moon rummaged through the wallet in the men's room as the traveler was boarding the plane. All but Mr. Ross O'Connor's license, a thousand dollars in cash, and credit and gas cards were thrown in the trash. Moon thought Mr. O'Connor must have been fairly well organized since he wrote the parking level and space in pen on the parking ticket.

The wallet also held a spare key, which was inserted into a business card-shaped piece of plastic. Moon would use it to open the door and start the car.

Moon thought, *I have never been so lucky as a thief,* as he walked into level four, parking space number 428. The 1985 Buick Riviera with RI plates sat in its assigned space in all its glory. He carefully placed the plastic key in the lock, and with a slight twist, the lock button rose upright.

He opened the door, placed his luggage in the back seat, and sat behind the wheel of his new acquisition. The ignition switch was a bit more demanding than the lock. However, by gently moving the steering wheel, the ignition released its grip, the plastic key turned, and the Buick came to life.

Moon drove down the four levels and handed the parking ticket to the attendant in the aluminum booth. On the attendant's sweatshirt, which was covered in food stains, "Parking Services" was stenciled across the front. He was about twenty to twenty-five years old. A tight Afro and a thick mustache covered an angular face. Moon couldn't tell if he was tall or short, fat or skinny, because he was bundled up in a sweatshirt with the hood up. He was encapsulated in an aluminum shell about the size of a phone booth with a radio blaring and the hum of an electric heater at his feet.

The attendant looked at the ticket. Then, he looked at Moon with an expression that said, "Buddy, you just parked here an hour ago. This is a long-term lot, moron."

Moon said he was just dropping off someone and ended up here instead of the short-term lot. This was exactly what Moon wanted; the attendant was just as disinterested in Moon as he was in his job. If ever questioned, he would have little memory of this encounter. Parking Services did not place a high priority on security. Moon was grateful for that and drove away without incident, relieved that his plan had worked.

"I still have to charge you for a full day," the young man said.

"No problem."

"Fifteen bucks," he said, staring straight ahead. Moon fished out a twenty, handed it over, and waited for the change. He considered a five-dollar tip but thought it might be something the kid would remember, and he didn't want that.

Leaving the parking lot after the wooden gate opened, Moon searched for signs pointing to Route 95 N. Hopefully in that direction lay a return to the life of organized crime.

30

GINO REMINISCES ABOUT UNCLE EARL

While Gino sat in front of his locker, the memory of his encounter with Michelle still haunted him. But in police work, there is no time for reflection. He was grateful, in fact, to return to work, and have his job to focus on.

It was just after 11:00 p.m. when he finished his twelve-hour shift. The cold of early spring woke up the barrack's boiler built in the 1920s. After decades of relying on coal, crude oil became its new lifeblood. Like a cranky old man begging for solitude, the boiler sounded angry.

After popping a couple of pain pills, perhaps to chase the final thoughts of Michelle away, Gino slowly stripped off his uniform and crawled into his bunk. State troopers were required to sleep at the barracks while off duty until the early 1970s. The bunks remained for troopers who were too weary to drive home after a fifteen-hour shift or were forced to stay because of a hurricane or blizzard. His mind was occupied with the day's events and sleep eluded him. The first part of Gino's day was routine; he assisted a stranded motorist, investigated two accidents, and issued two speeding tickets.

He received a radio call around twelve thirty in the afternoon. Hope Valley Barracks' radio call sign was K-3. In the northern part of the state, all the barracks were designated X, while in the southern part, they were referred to as K. Portsmouth was K-1, Wickford was K-2, and Hope Valley was K-3. The reasoning was never provided, but that was how it was done, so there would be no explanation forthcoming.

"K-3 to twenty-eight."

The words "twenty-eight" caught his ear immediately. No matter what the chatter on the radio was, Gino, like most cops, drowned it all out until his number was called. Gino and every other trooper were so wedded to their badge numbers that they were made part of everything numerical in their lives. License plates, telephone numbers, beeper numbers, flip phones, and alarm codes. Many troopers had no idea about the trooper whose number they had just been given, not so with Gino. His number was part of his family history.

Earl Peterson, Gino's uncle, joined the state police in 1952 and received badge twenty-eight. His law enforcement career began years earlier as a patrolman in East Providence. East

Providence was a suburb of Providence, and in the fifties, it was dotted with residential sections, some light industry, and many stores and restaurants. It was policed by a small department of fifteen officers.

Earl was assigned a midnight to 8:00 a.m. walking beat on Taunton Ave. between Interstate 195 and Pawtucket Ave., a distance of over two miles. After roll call, his sergeant would load two or three cops into his car and drive them to their routes to walk, observe, and replace night watchmen.

They carried guns, handcuffs, and a walking stick. Along with their uniform was a set of keys for most of the businesses. This set allowed them to lock doors when owners forgot, allowing them the luxury of dinner and a quiet night at home while the police protected their lives and property.

Perhaps the most significant part of their equipment was the key to their call boxes. In the fifties, there were no portable radios, only these boxes sprinkled throughout the city. They were hung on telephone poles and provided a direct link from the streets to the station. A communication device was made up of two switches, which resembled an electrical breaker, mounted exactly five feet five inches above the ground.

One switch alerted the station if an officer needed assistance. The other was to be pulled every two hours to let the station know you were doing your rounds. The sergeant would leave the cozy station to check on you if you missed the box, so you better have a compelling reason.

Earl, like most officers, did his job, but on cold winter nights, it was impossible to stay warm. Many officers let themselves into businesses to warm up, even though it was frowned upon.

Gino remembered a story his uncle used to tell about staying warm. While walking his beat one night, a wintry blend of rain and snow hit the city at 6:00 a.m. Leery of being caught by an early-arriving business owner, he looked elsewhere for shelter. A tractor-trailer parked behind a construction company caught his attention. In the back of the truck, Earl saw reams of insulation.

He crawled into the truck and resolved to warm up and get back to the station by eight o'clock. As every officer knows, working midnights is challenging because you're constantly trying to stay awake. By the time the sun rises, your body is crying for sleep. As a result, Earl fell asleep.

He was startled by the sounds of schoolchildren laughing and giggling as they waited for school. Trapped inside the truck, he prayed the sergeant wasn't out looking for him. He refused the embarrassment of exiting the truck in front of a group of kids.

Finally, they got on the bus, and Patrolman Earl Peterson emerged from the truck. He then walked to the station and was greeted by a barrage of foul language from his sergeant.

"Where the hell were you? We thought you were dead!"

Earl told him he had stopped at Jim's for breakfast before coming in.

"Sure, Peterson. And I have a date with Marilyn Monroe tonight. You're working a double tonight, so get back here in four hours."

During his time at the department, he watched state troopers patrol Route 44, which ran right through East Providence on its way to Providence.

His midnight to eight shifts took him along Taunton Ave., the city's main street. On cold winter nights, troopers would offer the young patrolman a seat in a warm car. In the summer, they would stop to talk when traffic was slow on the highways. Sharing stories about their departments, Earl learned what it was like to be a state trooper and decided that was the life he wanted to live.

During his next day off, he drove to Lincoln Barracks and applied for the next state police training academy.

Earl had once explained to Gino how the fifties were a time when police chiefs ruled over every aspect of an officer's life. An officer was once seen dating the chief's Catholic daughter, which was promptly ended when the chief forbade her from dating an Episcopalian.

The East Providence police chief was furious when he found out about Earl's application to the state police. Earl was called into his office and informed that if the state police called, he would not recommend him. Besides the inherent animosity most local chiefs had for the glorified highway patrol, he would not suffer the indignity of someone leaving his department for another.

Earl was dejected but determined, and he put all his efforts into impressing his chief. His opportunity came on a frigid January night while walking his beat at 2:00 a.m. As he walked down Hunt St., just off Taunton Ave., he saw smoke billowing from one of the three-decker houses.

There were no call boxes nearby for Earl. He kicked in the front door and screamed at the top of his lungs: "Fire! Get out! Fire! Get out!"

Earl led three families into the street and out of danger. Other than some smoke inhalation, everyone survived. Earl was covered in soot and his face blackened by smoke.

When he finally got to a box on Taunton Ave., the responding lieutenant told him: "You did a nice job, kid, but you look like shit. Get cleaned up at the station and start working on your report."

The next night, when he reported for duty, the chief was waiting for him. As he entered the chief's office, he was chewing on a large cigar and a layer of ashes covered his white shirt. He'd been chief for over twenty years and looked like Detective Andy Sipowicz of *NYPD Blue* on a bad day.

"Well, kid, I guess there's no holding you back now; you're a hero. I'm not going to stop you from joining the state police."

"Thank you, Chief," Earl said.

"Just so we are clear, if it doesn't work out with the state police you're never coming back here as long as I'm chief. Dismissed."

Gino was inspired by these stories to join the state police. But now he felt he had betrayed the legacy of his uncle, a hero who saved people, someone people would remember. At this rate, all Gino would be remembered for was being kicked out of the Intelligence Unit and not making a difference in his community.

31

LANGUAGE BARRIER

"Go ahead, K-3," Gino responded.

"Respond to the barracks. See Det. Coelho when you get here. He will be waiting for you."

Detective Felix Coelho was a relatively new member of the Intelligence Unit. A solid, five-foot-eight man, Felix wore a dark suit, white shirt, and green tie as well as the obligatory wingtip shoes. Across his waist, he wore handcuffs, a state police badge, and a snub nose .357.

Besides being fiercely proud of his Portuguese heritage, Felix also looked the part. He was a short, stocky man with the blackest hair Gino had ever seen. When you looked at his face, you were met with thick eyebrows over dark eyes that seemed skeptical but also confident.

Det. Coelho was a tenacious worker and not to be trifled with. He grew up on the streets of Providence's Portuguese section, known as Fox Point. He boxed in the Marine Corps and earned a Silver Star in Vietnam during a two-year stint.

"Gino, I need help arraigning two prisoners. Would you be able to assist me?" Felix asked.

Felix didn't mention Gino's stint in the Unit; he was a hard-working detective who never mistreated Gino. If you asked Felix, he would say he believed Gino was falsely blamed for having lost witnesses in the past, and it was not his mistake that cost the force an asset. That was why Felix kept in touch with Gino and was proud to call him a friend.

"Sure, Felix, whatever you need," Gino said eagerly, sounding like a rookie trying to get into the Intelligence Unit. He took away the rookie part and knew that was precisely what he was trying to do.

Felix grabbed a thick file folder and pulled out two arrest warrants. Felix and his partner had investigated a case of two Portuguese men taking advantage of new arrivals to the country. They would promise them driver's licenses for $500 a pop. If you weren't in the country legally, there was no written test, driving test, eye exam, or dealing with state officials.

Gino and Felix walked to the cell block and pulled out the two arrestees. They were mirror images of each other: small, dark, and wiry. Gino photographed them and fingerprinted them. Felix started speaking Portuguese rapidly. A series of guttural sounds delivered machine-gun-style gave Gino a slight sensation of throbbing in his temples.

Despite taking two five-hundred-milligram tablets already, it was time for another Vike. This would be sufficient to get through the arraignment.

Gino promised himself he would cut down to one-and-a-half pills for a week. Then he would cut down to one for a week, then half for a week, and then wean off the drugs completely. Gino's dream seemed more like a fantasy than a reality, almost like an empty promise from someone struggling with addiction. However, with faith and hard work, Gino's dream could come true. It can be difficult to hold onto this belief when surrounded by doubt.

Gino completed the process and handcuffed the defendants for the ride to court.

Felix told Gino: "They both cooperated and gave up a DMV supervisor who was giving them license blanks for the phony licenses. She charged them one hundred dollars for a blank. We'll arrest her next week."

As they placed the two men in the back of the cruiser, Felix continued the story. "I told them that if they plead guilty, the judge will put them on unsupervised probation for a year, and if they don't get in any trouble during the year, their records will be wiped clean. They liked it, so I told them the only English they needed to know was the word "guilty." I told them to say it when the judge asked for a plea, and I would take care of the rest."

The ride from Hope Valley to the District Court in Westerly was about thirty minutes. Gino could only hear the two men in the backseat practicing.

"Guilty . . . Guilty . . . Guilty," on and on all the way to the courthouse.

The foursome arrived at the Westerly district court around 9:45 a.m. just before the 10:00 a.m. arraignment. The courthouse was in an old brick building that looked like a medieval castle, complete with towers and a large front door spacious enough to drive a car through. Gino pulled into the rear parking lot where Felix and the prisoners were led into the courtroom.

At a typical initial arraignment, defendants are asked if they wish to plead guilty or not guilty. If they plead guilty, the arraigning officer would cite the facts of the case and a recommendation for sentencing. Then the judge would hand down a sentence. If the defendant pleads not guilty, a pretrial date is set, and the officer is asked for a bail recommendation.

"Gino," Felix said, "I don't want to take this to trial, and neither do they. Believe me, if we go to trial, this is no slam dunk. Getting a plea is the way we win this."

Prior to the court proceedings beginning, Det. Coelho delivered the two warrants to the court clerk while he led the defendants into the courtroom. He sat them in a row occupied by those living under the presumption of innocence, even if that presumption was a thin blanket.

During the session, Presiding Judge Terrence Houlihan informed all those who were to be arraigned of their rights. He then explained that he would accept a plea of guilty or not guilty in misdemeanor cases.

Judge Houlihan addressed all the arrestees: "If you are found responsible, you could receive a fine of up to $1,000 or up to a year in prison, depending on the charges you face. All felonies are automatically sent to Superior Court."

Felix and Gino then played the waiting game that every cop learns to play—the art of waiting for your case to be called by the judge. The wheels of justice turn either slowly or not at all. For a cop, waiting becomes an art form. Those who don't perfect it are doomed to hours of boredom and frustration. Gino would relive great childhood moments, recreate scenes from his favorite movie in his head, or think about his job, family, and what he would eat for lunch. Mental gymnastics were essential to ward off the boredom.

But today, Felix and Gino were in luck, and within fifteen minutes of arriving, the clerk called Jose Tavares to come forward and face the judge. As Det. Coelho took his place at the podium just off to the side of the judge's bench, Gino removed the handcuffs from defendant Tavares and placed him directly in front of the judge.

Separating the defendant from the judge's bench was a large table at which the clerk sat facing the defendant but never looking up. The clerk was always shuffling papers as the defendants walked up to the bench, much like the line at a takeout restaurant.

"Det. Coelho," Judge Houlihan said, causing Felix to recite the facts of the case and the charges levied against the defendants.

"Your honor, Mr. Tavares is charged with obtaining money under false pretenses. It is alleged that the defendant defrauded numerous individuals out of hundreds of dollars. RI driver's licenses were provided to victims without requiring them to undergo the legal process."

"As to your plea, Mr. Tavares?" the judge asked.

"Guilty!" replied Jose with all the confidence of Larry Bird shooting a free throw.

"I'll accept your guilty plea and sentence you to one year of unsupervised probation. You must also pay court costs and sign your paperwork before leaving the court. Next case."

The clerk motioned for Jose to stand to the side for a moment. This was so that she could call Manny to come forward since they were companion cases; the paperwork would be the same.

"Manny Soares," the clerk said, and Manny came forward.

Again, the judge began the ritual, and Felix repeated the same facts as he had for Jose and looked back up at the judge.

Judge Houlihan pulled the paperwork closer to his face and asked, "How do you plead, Mr. Soares?"

Soares, once confident, was panic-stricken. He slumped slightly and his shoulders sagged. His face was ashen, and his mouth was open, but no words came out. He rocked back and forth as the judge repeated, "How do you plead, Mr. Soares?"

Still nothing. The judge looked down at the defendant in frustration and sternly asked, "Mr. Soares, what is your plea?"

Again panic, more rocking and silence. The volume of chatter in the courtroom increased.

Suddenly, from the side of the courtroom, recently convicted defendant Jose Tavares screamed at the top of his lungs, "He guilty too!"

As laughter erupted throughout the courtroom, Judge Houlihan banged his gavel over and over but even the normally stoic court clerk was moved to near tears of laughter.

In response, Judge Houlihan vacated Jose Tavares's plea and set a two-week pretrial conference date with the public defender and a court-appointed interpreter. He did the same for Soares. The two were released on personal recognizance on the condition that they appear within two weeks.

After gathering up his paperwork, Detective Coelho left the courtroom.

"Nice try, Detective," the judge said. Felix nodded and left. Gino trailed behind him.

32

MOON'S RHODE ISLAND PAST
Winter 1989

With every mile north on Interstate 95, Moon came closer to his triumphant return or his ultimate demise. He had no idea which fate awaited him, but he had gone too far to turn back now. Although the odds were against him, Moon had returned to the family to reclaim his place.

And besides, he felt like he had his own reasons for flipping. Moon only became a witness for the state because he was in the unenviable position of doing time for a crime that he didn't commit. His boss Frank "Bobo" Detroia had forced him to go to trial in Massachusetts on charges of aggravated assault of a union official.

He was found guilty and sentenced to twenty to thirty years in Walpole State Prison in Massachusetts. Twenty to thirty years in his early fifties was a life sentence.

His first five years were spent wondering how he had ended up in that shithole with no hope of ever leaving it.

The soldiers of his Airborne division called it FUBAR, or getting your life fucked up beyond all recognition.

RI mob operations were heavily involved in labor unions, as were most mob operations on the East Coast. They controlled most aspects of unions, jobs, pensions, and contracts.

Creating no-show jobs was the goal. Positions where mobsters could report to work in the morning and sit around all day collecting a paycheck. However, Fall River's union leader was reluctant to sign this contract, which was favorable to the mob and the business owner.

The RI mob wanted quite the opposite. They would give the union a low wage increase in exchange for about a dozen no-show jobs for the mob. It would screw union members, but it would line the pockets of the mob.

Bobo had tried his best to sweet-talk the guy into agreeing to the contract, but he refused. If you run a mob crew, the currency of the realm is violence, to be employed with vigor when needed.

And so, it was decided that Frank Guerriero, president of Local 451 of the Laborers Union, would be persuaded to agree to the contract by the use of a baseball bat. Bobo ordered his chief leg breaker, Frank Martellini, to do the job, and he picked another one of his flunkies, Albino Pontarelli, to go with Frank.

The beating went well for the mob, not so much for Mr. Guerriero who ended up with many broken bones and a concussion. Since the job had "mob" written all over it, the Fall River Police Department contacted the Providence Police Department for help.

Fall River had been handed an incredible clue; the genius Martellini had used his own car to drive to Fall River, and a witness got the plate. When the name Martellini came up in the Providence detective squad room, it was mentioned in the same breath as Richard "Moon" Capelli, his close partner in crime.

The Providence Police showed the badly beaten Frank Guerriero two photo lineups, one with Moon's picture and one with Martellini's picture. Mr. Guerriero picked out Frank's picture right away, but he needed a little encouragement from the detectives to pick out Moon.

A carefully placed thumb on the "right" photo is sometimes all it takes. The thumb, in this instance, was provided by Det. Francis Wordell, a thirty-year veteran of the force who had spent his career trying to bring down Bobo's crew with little success. Wordell was old school. In his world, a little encouragement was in order.

Moon was responsible for running the mob's gambling operation, making him guilty of that and many other crimes that Wordell was never able to prove. Frustration can turn a cop bitter and willing not just to bend but to break the rules to make an arrest.

Guerriero looked up at Wordell's bloodshot eyes and pocked face and thought, *Screw these guys. Those guys almost beat me to death.* With shaking hands, he pointed out Moon.

Wordell grinned, and his yellow-stained teeth barely kept back the bad breath.

It took Moon two years of stewing in his cell until he turned his energies to getting out from under the sentence and the mob. The mob soon forgot him and left him to rot in his cell despite the promises to take care of him. He was left to fend for himself with no support or hope of release. He was a forgotten man, condemned to a life of misery and despair.

Whenever he thought of all the crimes he had been involved in with Bobo, his mind kept returning to the murder of Richard "Dickie" Calderone. As a member of the Raimondi crime family, Calderone had gotten out of control, so Bobo was ordered to kill him.

Bobo took advantage of the contract to secure himself an induction into the family as a full-fledged member of the mob. The mistake he made was describing the murder in full detail to his crew.

If Moon played it right, the RI State Police would believe he was involved in this ten-year-old murder case. His plan was elaborate and brilliant. He asked the state police to visit him in prison. The next day, they were there.

He told them he had seen Dickie Calderone's murder and gave them all the details of the hit Bobo had boasted about endlessly. In exchange for the state police's help in getting him out of his wrongful conviction, he offered to testify.

The state police believed him, and after months of investigation, they indicted many members of the mob. By the time they realized Moon had lied, they had Moon and two other witnesses in protective custody. Using Moon and the others, they made many cases against Detroia and his crew.

They could have sent him to jail for lying to the grand jury about the Calderone case. Instead, they cleared him of the wrongful conviction with the indictment of Albino Pontarelli, the real culprit in the beating. They then brought him back to the grand jury where he recanted his original lies.

After that, all the state wanted to do was get rid of him. One night, while sleeping in his room under the protection of the state police, two United States Marshals awoke him, and he disappeared into the Witness Protection Program.

Now he was headed back to Rhode Island to face the new boss of the Raimondi crime family. In prison, Moon was still serving his sentence when Pasquale Raimondi, the Old Man, passed away. Before he passed, the Old Man named his son, Louie "Little Knives" Raimondi, his successor.

Although Moon had turned against his family, he hoped to show Louie that his imprisonment for a crime he didn't commit justified his actions.

Moon thought he was also still valuable. He hoped Louie would recall that Moon was the leading bookmaker for the family, running their entire business. This was a bold undertaking, and he was probably going to end up in the trunk of a car. If they killed him, he thought, it was better than living his life as a fucking security guard in Falls Church.

On the radio, Whitney Houston sang "I Want to Dance with Somebody" as his plan rattled around in his head. When he returned to Providence, his fate would be determined by the mob. But Moon was a betting man. He decided to take advantage of some female companionship before he sank his head into the lion's jaws.

Whitney told Moon that she wanted to be with someone, so Moon pressed down on the accelerator. As a result of the song, he became more determined to "be with someone."

33

MOON'S WESTERLY ADVENTURE

The rest of Moon's life, however short, would be shaped by what he did now. He had to make the right decision. He had to make a move that guaranteed his safety. He had to act quickly. With no time to spare, Moon was determined to make a decision that would secure his future and preserve his life.

As a diversion, he headed to Westerly, Rhode Island, before spinning the wheel of fortune. There, he hoped to find refuge from the dangers lurking in the shadows. He was determined to start anew, but little did he know that he was about to stumble into a world of mystery and intrigue. He soon realized that even in Westerly, he wasn't safe from the darkness that had been chasing him for so long.

Westerly was a bucolic resort town with picturesque beaches and a boardwalk area reminiscent of Atlantic City. The large boardwalk framed the beach with shops, restaurants, bars, and tourist shops. White cabanas dotted the sand, and the beach staff were all attired in blue Bermuda shorts and polo shirts emblazoned with "Watch Hill Beach and Surf Club."

Moon fondly remembered another side of Westerly that most residents would be appalled to know existed. Many years ago, Bobo had learned of a high-priced brothel operated out of an old Victorian house on the outskirts of town.

He checked with Pasquale Raimondi, the boss at the time, and learned that it was not under the protection of anyone in the family and, therefore, fair game.

After a few meetings, the madam agreed to engage Bobo and his crew for protection in return for a modest 10 percent of the profits. In addition, she agreed to provide the free services of any of the young ladies under her employ.

Moon took the last exit before the Connecticut border and headed south on Route 3, the main route into Westerly. As he drove, he wondered if the brothel was still running after Bobo and his crew had been eliminated. Was it under someone else's protection? Would they know his story? Would they care?

In Moon's world, there were two ways to find a prostitute: ask a cab driver or visit a local watering hole and ask the bartender.

"Welcome to Westerly," the sign brightened his mood as he envisioned a delightful diversion from his potentially life-ending mission. Route 3 became Main Street, and he pulled into the Amtrak station parking lot just on the outskirts of the center of town.

A brick building with large windows framed with black metal awnings and black faux gas streetlamps surrounded the parking lot. He walked into the station and picked up a copy of the *Providence Journal* to check on the local news. Moon thought it would be wise to be aware of what was happening in his hometown.

Providence's mayor was under fire, accused of corruption. A state representative was arrested for DUI. There was an accusation of child molestation against a parish priest. Apparently, not much had changed since he left. He soon became bored with the paper and began watching people instead.

As a result of spending so much time on the streets and in the can, Moon learned the importance of studying people in order to survive. Observation was an amazing way to figure out whether someone was a threat. Besides, it was fun to guess the story. What was their destination? How did they make a living?

He saw students returning to the University of Rhode Island, which was about thirty minutes away. A young couple arrived with luggage perhaps to be married at Ocean House, a converted 1800s mansion.

A short, fat, dark-haired, middle-aged man stood on a corner wearing a blue shirt and a Red Sox ball cap. He wore jeans and sneakers, and his belt loop was adorned with a chain holding too many keys. Moon's instincts would be shocked if the guy wasn't a cab driver.

When he approached the man, Moon said, "Taxi."

"At your service," the cabbie said.

Moon decided to cut to the chase, "Is that house of comfort still on Burnside Street?"

The man took a step back and said, "You a cop?"

"Do I look like a cop, asshole?" Moon answered sharply. By the driver's response he knew at once his instincts were still intact.

The driver fumbled with the keys, looked around, and whispered, "Yup, but the fare is fifty dollars."

Moon replied, "No, I'm pretty sure it's twenty-five."

As he pointed at his yellow cab, the taxi driver grunted. In the car, Moon worried he had made a foolish decision to return to a house of prostitution controlled by the mob. Is there a mob soldier inside the house watching over the girls and the money?

Roxie Vitale, the granddaughter of an old-time mobster, ran the house when Bobo's crew controlled it. His crew trusted her not to let anyone into the house that she didn't know. Bobo also knew how much money he should receive from the house every week. If he didn't get his cut, she would drown in the Atlantic.

Moon noticed the Victorian-style house's siding had been covered in gaudy yellow vinyl. Street-facing bay windows were made of stained glass. About an acre of land was meticulously maintained around the house, which was surrounded by a four-foot-high New England stone wall.

Other than the two cars with out-of-state license plates, there wasn't a hint of what was going on inside the house. Moon jumped out of the car, paid the cabbie, and walked up to the house on the gravel path. He rang the doorbell and waited.

Roxie opened the door, and she was still a knockout even though it had been about ten years. She had a striking appearance with her tall figure, red hair, and amber eyes. She had a certain air of confidence about her, and people were drawn to her. She carried herself with grace and poise, and she was always the center of attention. Her dress was elegant, and the jade necklace around her neck added a touch of sophistication.

Moon was unable to speak for a moment, but he regained his composure and said, "Hello, Roxie, do you remember me? I was a very close friend of Bobo."

She smiled politely and lied, "I'm sorry, sir, but I don't remember you. Frank had many friends visit over the years; it's nearly impossible to remember them all."

Moon wondered why she was playing dumb, and then it hit him: *I'm a rat, and memories had not faded as he had hoped. Okay if that's the way it's going to be, I'll just play along.*

"May I come in?" he asked.

"Yes, please step inside." After turning her back, Moon followed her into the foyer. The dark carpet and curtains overwhelmed him as he looked around. In the center of the room, there was a chandelier. Right next to the closed pocket doors was a small desk.

"Name?" the madam asked.

"Come on, Richard Capelli!" he said with disdain.

The madam softly asked, "Are you a member? This is a member-only club."

Moon started to stutter, "What the hell are you talking about, member, member . . ."

"Sir, sir, it appears you are upset. Please step through the doors and someone will help you," she said as she pulled open the pocket doors.

As Moon walked into the larger room, he continued to feel a sense of knowing that this was not a place to cause a scene. He was on the floor before he had a chance to react, tripped by a massive combat boot.

While lying on the ground, he was kicked several times and covered his head to avoid being knocked out. He was flipped over onto his back and a large bore weapon was stuck in his face. Holding his hands up, he waited for the gun to click.

Instead, a familiar voice called out. The sound was deeper than he recalled. "Uncle Moon, is that you?"

34

THE ONE THAT GOT AWAY
Ten Years Ago

Gino had just finished compiling the report of a hit-and-run incident on Route 95 N at Route 117 in Warwick. A Chevrolet Chevelle had collided with another vehicle while it was sitting in construction traffic and then fled the scene. The victim of the accident provided Gino with as much of a description as possible, but it wasn't much. Another motorist who witnessed the accident also provided additional information. Gino then relayed the details to the trooper on the desk, who repeated the information over the interstate radio, a channel for all police departments to communicate. As Gino pondered the likelihood of finding the car, his thoughts drifted back to 1979.

Every cop is haunted by an unsolved case. In small doses, it consumes them, like the drip-drip from a leaky faucet. The result is self-doubt. Is there anything I could have done differently? Did I miss anything? I have to tell the victim's family again and again that there is nothing new to report.

Gino was haunted by one case in particular. He had tried to solve it for months but could not resolve it. He felt like he had failed the victim and that this case reflected his own shortcomings as an investigator. More important, this case brought back memories of his father's death, which haunted him as much as the Jason Paul case.

Gino rolled down all four windows of his cruiser as he rolled down Route 95 in the summer heat of July. The moment he approached Thurber Avenue, where Jason Paul had been killed, he was reminded of the tragedy that took place on that day. It happened in July of 1979 when Gino was new to the Intelligence Unit.

Paul was a kid who grew up in his neighborhood. The Beach Boys' song about their Chevy 409 reminded him of Jason's love for cars. Jason saved up enough money to buy a Chevy Cheville when he was just sixteen years old. He was the envy of his neighborhood because he always drove around in new cars until he wrapped one around a telephone pole on Dean St. It turned out that he had stolen it from outside a restaurant on Atwells Ave.

Back in 1979, troopers on the scene of the hit-and-run fatality contacted the Intelligence Unit because the car was stolen, and the operator was known to them as an associate of the Raimondi family. Gino and his partner Don Kennedy responded. They were sent to the scene because Jason was known for stealing cars for the mob. Around 8:00 p.m., they arrived at the crime scene on Route 95 at the Thurbers Ave. curve in Providence.

The relatively straight highway was curved to the right, then to the left, before straightening again as it approached Pawtucket, a city north of Providence. The lack of logic behind the curve of the highway was only surpassed by the equally infamous "S" curves in Pawtucket. It was literally a serpentine highway that snaked through this industrial metropolis.

At the curve, several cruisers and rescue wagons were visible. Against the Jersey barrier was a red '78 Ford Escort sedan. The rear end of the car had exploded, and a tire had landed in the breakdown lane. Gino and Donald walked to the front of the sedan from behind the cruiser. Waiting for detectives and the medical examiner to arrive, the troopers covered the body with a tarp.

Gino said, "Oh, shit, that's Jason," as Donald removed the tarp. They looked down at the mangled body of Jason Paul, a young man in his mid-to-late twenties. There was no damage to his face, but his body was completely destroyed. "It looks like he has been hit by a truck," Gino murmured in disbelief.

Putting on rubber gloves, Gino and Donald surveyed the accident scene and then called for crime scene technicians. Don pulled out the victim's wallet from the back pocket of his jeans. The license belonged to Jason Paul of Narragansett. Sgt. Bartley, the uniformed supervisor at the scene, gave Gino and Donald the unenviable task of notifying Jason's family.

35

DEATH NOTIFICATION

The Town of Narragansett is a seaside community made up of tracks of housing, restaurants, shops, and some of the most picturesque beaches in the state. Its location at the southernmost point on Narragansett Bay brought tourists, URI students, and fishermen.

Gino and Donald arrived at 210 Greenbriar Lane at about 2:00 a.m. The house was in a cul-de-sac within walking distance of a large sidewalk and a cement wall that hugged the coastline for miles. The gambrel house boasted a rich brown exterior accented by vibrant yellow trim, which now appeared slightly weathered and worn. Enclosed by a sturdy stone wall, the property featured a gravel driveway that meandered gracefully toward the front door. As they drove down the driveway, the motion detector caused a light to come on and flood the front of the house.

They got out of the detective car, switched on the emergency lights in the grill, and headed to the front door. As they approached, a man in his fifties opened the door. He saw Gino and Donald in their suits and ties and shiny shoes. At the sight of the detectives, his knees buckled—a sign to Gino and Donald that he was anticipating the news they would deliver.

His wife appeared in a bathrobe on their staircase as Gino and Donald helped him up and guided him into the living room. Wearing a quizzical expression on her face, she witnessed her husband being held up by the two detectives. It was a look that seemed to implore: Please spare me the details I already suspect.

Donald said, "I'm Det. Kennedy, and this is my partner, Det. Peterson. Are you Jason Paul's parents?"

"Yes," the father said, and his wife slowly moved to the couch where she joined her husband.

Donald spoke softly. "I'm sorry to inform you that Jason was killed in a car accident tonight."

Cassie Paul began to wail, burying her head into the arms of her husband. Edmond and Cassie Paul were living the most horrific nightmare. Their lives would never be the same.

Gino and Donald tried to obtain as much information about Jason as possible while the Pauls cursed the creator and clung to each other.

"Mr. Paul, can you tell us a little bit about your son?"

A grimace crossed Mr. Paul's face as he spoke. "He was a kind boy, never a problem for me or for his mother."

"Never?" Gino asked.

"OK, sure, he got into some trouble with cars, joyriding that sort of thing, nothing serious." Mr. Paul's eyes darted away from Gino and to his wife.

Gino had more questions, but now was not the time. He decided to save them for later and instead focus on the task at hand. He knew that discretion was the better part of valor, and he didn't want to risk offending anyone or asking the wrong question. It was his intention to get the job done, and he would ask Mr. Paul about Jason's organized crime connections later.

Gino turned his attention to Edmond and spoke. "Is there someone you can call to help your wife? If you like, we can call the EMTs to come over. They might be able to help her calm down."

Ed said, "Thanks, but I'm about to call my daughter because she lives ten minutes away."

"Was he married?" Donald asked.

"No, he was single and lived here with his mom and me. We've lived here since we moved out of Providence ten years ago. He lived here with his brother and sister."

"It's time to call Devin and Mary Beth," he said, reaching out to his wife. She lost what color remained on her face as her dreams of his wedding and grandchildren crumbled.

"What happened to Jason?" she screamed repeating the question to herself. Donald told her the story. "He was on 95 in Providence. Jason had pulled over against the Jersey barrier in the high-speed lane. He was struck by someone."

"Did you get the bastard?" Ed asked.

Gino replied, "I'm sorry, but the driver left the scene. We're looking for the car as we speak."

Ed said, "You mean they hit my son and didn't stop. Just left him there?"

"I'm afraid so. I promise you we will do everything we can to catch this guy."

Cassie whispered, "But that won't bring my Jason back, Detective."

"I'm sorry, ma'am, you're right. It won't," Gino said softly.

Donald said to Ed: "Mr. Paul, before we leave, do you mind if we look in Jason's room? The more info we have the better."

"Sure, go ahead. Upstairs, down the hall, second door on the right."

Gino has seen all the movies and TV shows where cops go into the victim's room and find that one piece of evidence that breaks the case. Cops know that rarely happens.

Despite knowing that finding the proverbial "smoking gun" that would help them solve a hit-and-run was the longest of shots, Donald and Gino were taught to follow procedure.

It's amazing what you can learn about a person in the room where they lay their head, the room that is their sanctuary, where closing the door closes out all the insanity of the world.

Jason's room was neat and uncluttered. The decor was an homage to Star Trek. Figurines and bobbleheads of Kirk, Scotty, Uhura, and Spock took up the top of his bureau.

In his closet, he kept a Starfleet academy uniform. Don fired up Jason's IBM XT, but there was nothing useful. They came downstairs to find more family gathered. Devin, Jason's younger brother, appeared stunned as if he had been near the explosion of a grenade.

Mary Beth, his older sister was huddled in the arms of her husband. Their eight year old had no idea what was going on and was trying to get someone to play a game with him. He carried his Chutes and Ladders game around the room fervently trying to get someone to pay attention to him.

There were neighbors. Some were crying, others stunned, and the stronger among them comforted the weaker. In a quick goodnight, Gino and Don promised to keep them posted.

In the weeks that followed, Don and Gino checked body shops, emergency rooms, and impound lots in hopes of finding a car with damage on its left side.

The crime scene technicians collected some green paint chips at the scene and sent them to the FBI crime lab in Washington. It could take many weeks to receive a response. The technicians identified the green paint chips as belonging to a 1974 Chevy Impala 500.

Don and Gino would spend a great deal of their time driving through large parking lots looking for a green Chevy Impala 500. Over the summer, they would use their own time to drive through parking lots at large malls and along state and town beaches.

They interviewed Jason's friends. Many of them were involved in his car theft ring and remained silent. It was true that Jason was killed, but it had nothing to do with stealing cars, according to one of Donald's informants. It was more about Jason disrespecting a made guy in a bar. Being embarrassed in front of a crowd did not go down well. The informant said that Jason had to be silenced for the sake of the made guy's reputation. Gino and Donald could not find any evidence to back up the informant's story, but they had to consider it. Every avenue they tried to follow to connect the mob to Jason's death led nowhere.

They would also review records of hit-and-runs in other states. As time passed, they made fewer and fewer calls. In addition, the number of newly filed cases never stopped. Then, there were transfers, promotions, and reassignments. Other than his family, only Gino and Donald would be plagued by the lack of closure as the weeks turned into months and months into years.

History repeating itself haunted him deeply, and he could not stop thinking about it. Jason Paul's case had many similarities. An unsolved motor vehicle accident involving mob overtones. Like his father's death, Jason Paul's involved a hit-and-run driver who had never been identified and a suspicious lack of witnesses. It was also suspected that organized crime was involved, as the accident occurred near a known mob hangout.

36

FAMILY REUNION
Winter 1989

Moon's nephew stood well over six feet tall with a muscular build. He sported close-cropped hair, a bit longer at the top. He wore a short leather jacket trimmed in red, a white casual shirt, and dark jeans. He resembled John Travolta from *Saturday Night Fever* but without the leisure suit.

Moon looked up. "Aldo, is that you?"

"Yeah, it's me Unc. You're lucky I didn't pistol whip you. Roxie thought you were going to try to rip us off. What the hell are you doing here?"

"No, no, Aldo, just looking for a little companionship . . . before I go to Providence and see the boss."

Aldo couldn't quite believe what he was hearing, "See the boss? Are you crazy? They all call you a rat. Do you know what will happen to you if you just show up?"

Aldo reached down with a large hand and yanked Moon up from the floor. Moon shook the fear from his body.

Ever the jokester, Moon answered, "I'll probably end up in a trunk, so that's why I stopped here first."

"Zio, I never could hate you because you were a rat, but others don't believe Bobo screwed you, and they hate you."

Moon continued, "I know, but that was a long time ago. Now I want back in the game."

Aldo was confused. "There was a fifty-thousand-dollar bounty on your head, and as far as I know, it's still there. Even my dad told us we couldn't have anything to do with you. We all kept a low profile when you were testifying."

"How is my brother? I've missed him."

"He's fine. He's still working in the bakery. But he never talks about you, and we're not allowed to mention you either. You're dead to him. Sorry."

Moon was crestfallen.

A butcher by trade, Moon's brother, Peter, was the kind of man the mob never bothered with because he was a civilian in their eyes. He worked at the Columbus Market in Providence which was popular with Italian immigrants. In addition, it was at the center of New England's organized crime network.

When Moon closed his eyes and breathed deeply, he could smell, hear, and see the market in his mind. A center of life on the hill, the market was stocked with cheeses of every kind and large cuts of meat hanging behind the deli counter. His brother's arguments with customers about which cut was best for them were less about anger and more about entertainment. The shelves were stocked with specialty foods, sauces, breads, and condiments, including virgin olive oil, the nectar of Italian cuisine.

"Zio, Zio," Aldo called out to Moon, shaking him out of his trip down memory lane.

"What?"

"You gotta get out of here ASAP. I'm really not sure what would happen to you if the boss found out."

Moon shook his head. "No matter how crazy it sounds, I want him to find out. But first, I have some questions."

"I'll be at the Bradford Café around 8:00 p.m. to answer your questions. Do you know where it is?" Aldo asked.

"Sure, right down the street, about a block from here. I just need a ride back to my car. I took a cab here from the train station."

"I'll take you back to your car, but remember, if you ever return to the family or ask to return, and it doesn't work out, we never met. If you tell them about our brief reunion here, they'll put me in cement overshoes. Capisce?"

Moon knew he was speaking like a mobster rather than a nephew when he said that.

"Capisce," Moon answered. "See you at the Bradford."

37

MOON AND ALDO AT THE BRADFORD

The Bradford Café was a bar above the former St. Louis hotel, now a boarding house. Moon arrived at the bar at about 7:45 p.m. He walked into the bar, which was surprisingly clean, well-lit, and filled with young people and workers from area businesses. So much for the dingy, dimly lit bar with dirty floors and an old man nursing his beer that he was expecting.

There was country music playing on the jukebox. Moon smirked at the irony of Hank Williams Jr. singing about family traditions. He headed to a booth, and the waitress came by. He ordered the local favorite, Narragansett draft beer. Not much had changed as far as beer was concerned, as change did not come easily to the inhabitants of Rhode Island.

At 8:00 p.m., Aldo walked in. He had changed into a soft brown leather coat, red T-shirt, and jeans rolled up just past his ankles. Moon thought, What a handsome bastard. Looks just like me.

The waitress came to the table and Aldo asked for an Old Fashioned. Mobsters drink beer and shots of whiskey. When his nephew ordered the drink, it didn't scream Mafia to him; it must be a phenomenon of the younger generation.

Aldo leaned in as they waited for the waitress to return and asked, "Unc, what's going on? You know I could get killed just sitting here with you. God forbid my father finds out."

"Look, kid, I don't want to get you in trouble. I just need a few answers, and then I'm out of here." As Moon spoke, he kept an eye on the door. While he trusted his nephew, even that trust had limitations.

"Okay, then shoot. I'll answer what I can. Just remember I'm a soldier. I work for a capo, so I'm not privy to what goes on."

Moon took a deep breath and started, "When I left, Pasquale was in charge, but I heard when I was in the joint he passed away and anointed his son."

"Unc, you know the Commission runs all the families in New York City, and they called the shots for New England. Louie, the Old Man's son, was backed by the Commission. So, he got the nod."

Moon thought for a minute, he remembered Louie was taken in by the Colombo family and lived and worked in New York. Pasquale sent him to NYC to lay low after he drove the car on one of the hits Pasquale ordered. Two bookies refused to kick back a percentage of the book to Pasquale, and they paid with their lives. He remembered that hit and Louie Raimondi leaving for NYC.

Aldo added, "Apparently, Louie hid out for a while, and he earned money for the Columbos, and they loved him. He even ended up settling a few beefs between the families."

"Louie 'Little Knives', right?" Moon asked.

"He's the one. They say he got the nickname because he sliced up some young punks at a bar. Unc, get it? But people now call him Mr. Raimondi or boss instead."

Moon thought back to the time when he first hooked up with the mob. Louie "Little Knives" was a young, up-and-coming gangster working for Tommy Cabralli, one of Pasquale's capos. Pasquale anointed his son as a soldier in the family after he killed the leader of an auto theft operation.

Jimmy O'Shea, the leader of the ring, was the leader of a burglary ring based in Pawtucket, an industrial city north of Providence. Jimmy's specialty was luxury jewelry and cracking safes for cash. Pasquale was fine with all of this. However, they weren't bringing the jewelry to Pasquale's fence, Andy "The Blind Pig" Rosette. The boss had warned them that if they failed to pay their respects, there would be consequences. The gang members knew this, but they didn't expect the boss to be so ruthless. They were in for a rude awakening as they soon found out what the consequences were.

O'Shea was found burned to a crisp in a stolen Cutlass Supreme in the woods at the Rhode Island-Massachusetts border between Pawtucket and Attleboro. He was slumped over the wheel, his foot pegging the gas pedal to the floor. The catalytic converter ignited some leaves under the car, and it burst into flames. The crime scene unit processed the scene after firefighters were able to douse the flames. The medical examiner took the charred remains for an autopsy and eliminated the possibility of an accidental end to O'Shea's career. The medical examiner ruled O'Shea was shot in the back of the head two times and died instantly.

As Moon looked at Aldo, he said, "Listen to me. Remember what happened to this kid. Stay sharp because when they come for you, they will most likely be your best friend. You won't feel suspicious. He will always sit behind you. That might just save your life one day."

"I won't put myself in that kind of situation. If I get jammed up, I'll just keep my mouth shut and do the time."

Aldo said this with the bravado of someone who has never done time in prison. He may think that his plan to remain silent was a wise one. Moon had tried that, however, and he couldn't take it, so he doubted that Aldo could.

"In today's world with RICO, guys are facing big numbers and singing like birds. It's not like the old days when everyone followed the rules. A family head was shot in the streets. There is no respect for bosses."

"Who's RICO?" Aldo asked.

Moon suddenly knew he would never see his nephew on *Jeopardy*. "RICO is not a guy, stupido. It's the federal law that allows prosecutors to target and prosecute organized crime. They use it to destroy entire families."

"What would you want me to do, then? Rat like you did?"

"Out of love for you, I will keep my temper in check. I told you why I had to do what I did, but this isn't about me, it's about you," he said.

He would do anything to protect his brother's son. This was the only way for him to feel that he was still part of his brother's life.

"If you get jammed up, listen to me, even if you don't want to play along. There's only one person I want you to talk to if something happens: Gino Peterson, the trooper from the neighborhood. He's a good man, and he'll help you out. He's from our neighborhood, so he knows what it's like. Just tell Gino the truth, no matter what. Gino understands this life of ours."

"Why him and not a lawyer? That's the rule." Aldo asked.

Moon ran his hand through his hair. "The lawyer is paid for by the mob, he's not there for your best interest. He's there to protect the boss and keep you from testifying."

"Why call Peterson?" Aldo asked.

Moon reached across the table and took his nephew's hands into his own, "Look, he kept me safe for the two years when I was in custody. He's a straight shooter. He's always honest and direct. Gino doesn't beat around the bush. He's reliable and dependable, and you can trust his word. There's no bullshit in him, and he's a helluva cop."

38

THE PLAN

The waitress returned with Aldo's drink and another draft beer for Moon. "I thought you might need another." She turned her head to the side and smiled.

Moon smiled back and nodded in appreciation. He raised the glass, thanked the waitress, and took a sip. The cold beer tasted refreshing, and he took his time to enjoy it. Moon's smile widened, and he gave the waitress a wink. She giggled and blushed before turning away to serve other customers. He watched her walk away, admiring her graceful movements.

Moon smiled and reminded himself to leave a big tip; after all, you never know what might happen. If you're not in there pitching, someone else will be.

"Aldo, don't you understand?" Moon snapped. "I was tried for a crime I did not even commit. Instead of taking the plea deal that the district attorney in Bristol County offered us, Frank Martellini thought he could win the case at trial. Despite not committing the crime, I was willing to accept the deal."

"With good behavior, I could have gotten out of jail in three years, maybe sooner. You know how liberal things are in Massachusetts. But that lughead Marty thought we could beat the case. Bobo followed along with it, and I had no choice but to do what my boss ordered."

"What job are you talking about? Why were you arrested?" Aldo asked.

"Bobo had a union in Fall River where he took a piece of the retirement fund, built no-show jobs into the contracts, and held the owner of the factory by the balls with the threat of a strike.

"Well, the contract with the union was close to ending so Bobo negotiated a sweetheart deal with the owner. Just a five-cent-an-hour increase for the union and a half dozen no-show jobs for our crew. The only fly in the ointment was the union president who wouldn't play along with the sham contract and started making noise," Moon said.

"So, what the hell happened to get you jammed up?" Aldo asked.

"In order to make the union guy cave, Bobo gives Marty the task of scaring him. He asked me if I would come with him. I was running the crew booking operations and Marty wanted to go there on Tuesday, which is my collection day, so I begged off. He asked Pontarelli, and the kid agreed.

"Let me tell you something about Marty and Pontarelli. Their combined IQs would not reach double digits. So, these two Einsteins drive up in Marty's car, wait outside the guy's house, and beat him with a baseball bat to within an inch of his life."

"I thought they were just supposed to scare him, right?" Aldo asked.

"They were, and Bobo was pissed when they got back and told him what they did," Moon replied. "It was a slam dunk for the cops because the union guy and a neighbor got the license plate of Marty's car."

"But how did you get pinched?"

"I swear the cop put his finger on my picture when they showed it, I bet it was that asshole Wordell who always had it in for me. He knew Marty and I were close," Moon said. "I swear the guy didn't have a life and just lived to screw with our crew." Moon took a large gulp of his beer. "They showed a lineup to the union guy, gave him a fuckin' hint, and he picked me."

"That sucks! Who was this cop? I don't remember him," Aldo replied.

Moon burped. "You wouldn't. He ate his gun just after he retired. He was a big guy, barrel-chested with a big head and a crew cut out of the fifties. He spent his off time at a bar on Broadway outside of Olneyville. Never married, never seen him with a broad, lived in a one-bedroom apartment. He was a loser."

"Hey, it gets better. Instead of taking a plea, we go to trial for assaulting a union official and extortion. The jury returned a guilty verdict in thirty minutes. The judge sentenced us to twenty-five years in prison. They hung me out to dry, even when they knew I was innocent."

"What do you need from me, Zio?" Aldo asked, finally understanding.

"Just tell me where I can find Louie, and I'll take it from there."

Aldo thought for a minute and said, "He's still working out of the back office of his business on Atwells Ave., but you'll never get inside because he always has two or three guys in front."

"Aldo, I'm off to see him. I told you I'd rather get gunned down than end up back in the protection program," Moon's voice rose an octave.

"Hey, slow down, Zio. Slow down a minute. Listen to your nephew," Aldo said, his nose flaring. His words were short and direct.

"There is one way you might be able to talk to him and not get yourself killed. Louie walks around Lincoln Woods Park every morning at 6:00 a.m. I had driven him up there a few times. The way it works was I parked in the parking lot, and he got out and walked around the lake. They don't tell you much except don't move until he gets back in the car. One time it took nearly two hours for him to return to the car. I had to stay in the same spot the entire time. He might have other security on the route, but I don't know. The boss is nuts. He might have guys in camos hiding in the woods!"

"I remember the park," Moon said. "It's just outside Providence. It's jammed in the summer with people from the city trying to escape the heat. There is a road that circles the entire park."

"Right, but at six o'clock in the morning, it's quiet except for the other walkers. If I were you, I'd start doing the same thing. Don't approach him right away. You can start off with a good morning or the weather. This will let him get used to seeing you."

"What if he recognizes me?" Moon asked.

"You were in the military, right? So what happens before every mission?"

"Recon," Moon responded.

"Right, check it out first. You'll find a tunnel that runs under the highway out of the park and over to a road that is parallel to the highway. Park your car there when you start walking in the morning. When you eventually approach him, make sure you're near the tunnel," Aldo said. "If he makes you, run through the tunnel, jump into your car, and drive to South America because you're fucked. Got it?"

"Got it," Moon said.

Aldo stood, gave Moon a hug, and kissed him on the cheeks. He slipped an envelope full of cash into his uncle's chest. As he walked away, *"In bocca al lupo."*

"Crepi il lupo," he replied. Moon couldn't help but laugh at the irony. Aldo's goodbye was an Italian idiom for good luck, but its literal translation was "In the wolf's mouth." Moon was headed to a meeting where he would basically be putting his head into the mouth of the Alpha wolf of the RI mob. Irony doesn't even come close.

39

OPERATING A GAMBLING OPERATION

Moon drove out of Westerly in the car he had stolen from the lot at Green Airport. As he headed up Route 95, he knew it was time for a new one.

Aldo suggested a salvage yard on Allens Ave. in Providence where he could buy a car. He gave his uncle two thousand dollars at the bar so he could buy a car and leave town if necessary.

While driving north, Moon passed through rural southern areas of the state. He then drove through Warwick, Cranston, and Providence. The state becomes more industrial as you travel north. Taking a deep breath of city air, Moon recalled his past.

He watched the gangsters growing up on the Hill who had cash, stylish clothes, and expensive cars, but never worked a legit job. Moon's two-year stint in the Army was his attempt to escape that life. After being medically discharged because of his bad back, he had no job opportunities, so he ran numbers for Paul "The Beak" Lottero, a neighborhood bookie. Making fifty dollars a week was easy. In every corner of the neighborhood, Moon collected slips from bookies.

Every Tuesday, The Beak gave his winnings to each bookie and collected any losses. His commission was 20 percent, and the bookies paid for his protection and assistance in collecting bets from reluctant losers. Eighty percent of the 20 percent was kicked upstairs to Pasquale.

Along the way, Moon learned that being a bookie was more than just collecting bets and hoping that you collected more losing bets than winning ones.

"Listen, kid, the whole idea is to get as close as possible to 50/50 on winning and losing bets," The Beak told him.

"Then how do you make money if everything is equal?" Moon asked.

"Look, we always collect ten dollars for every hundred-dollar bet. Let's call those ten dollars a service fee. On the streets, they call it vigorish and don't ask. I have no idea why they call it the vig."

"Why? Isn't it in the latest edition of the Mafia dictionary?" Moon clowned.

"Funny, Moon Pie," The Beak continued. "Let's make the rest simple. If dummy #1 bets a hundred and he wins, we give him two hundred."

"Where do you get the hundred to pay him?" Moon asked, then thought for a minute. "From the loser, right?"

"Right," The Beak replied.

"But that only works if you have an equal number of bets on both the winning and losing side, right? I mean, I know we're going to collect on the losing bets, but there's no way we're going to have all the loser bets," Moon said.

"Then we're going to have to do something about those losing bets to make money. Suppose the Patriots are playing the Jets. Forget about the odds, just concentrate on winning and losing bets right now. The rest will come later.

"Because people are crazy about the Patriots, I anticipate a lot of action on them. If the Pats win, I'm screwed. Unless . . ." He just let that last part just hang out there, testing Moon.

"Unless you find someone with a ton of Jets bets, and you exchange bets," Moon said. Numbers were always his strong suit, and it showed.

The Beak was impressed with the kid's answer. "Pretty sharp, kid. Personally, you could be on *Jeopardy* until Alex asks you what you do for a living. We give the winner his two hundred dollars. We keep the loser's bet and the vig. There you go, we just made ten bucks on one bet. Multiply that by thousands of bets."

Moon chimes in, "So who cares who wins or loses the game? Just collect those service fees and throw in some extra losing bets and it's like having a license to print money."

"You know what they say, kid, the house never loses," The Beak said.

"Amen to that," Moon replied.

"Hey, Moon shot, listen, you're smart with numbers, you're good with paperwork, and you're not afraid of hard work. You got a future in this business if you want it."

"I want it," Moon said.

"All right," The Beak said. "There are some critical rules to follow. Some might even say they are lifesaving. It is never, ever, ever a wise idea to skim off the top. Stealing from me is stealing from the boss, and that's a death sentence, my friend."

"What's the second rule?" Moon asked.

"Don't be like these bookies who become degenerate gamblers. I'm not saying don't gamble because if you didn't like gambling, you wouldn't be in this business. But once you lose everything gambling, you skim off the top and that's fatal. Lesson over."

40

A NEW CAR FOR MOON

About two in the afternoon, Moon pulled into the scrapyard along the Providence River. The river emptied directly into the Narragansett Bay. Filled with cars of all sizes and shapes, the yard covered two blocks of this prime Providence waterfront. This was a city that had once relocated a river as part of revitalization. Yet, the waterfront scrap piles and mostly abandoned railways remained a scar on the city's potential. The yard's location—at the beginning of one of the most picturesque bays in the country—was the perfect example of Rhode Island politics. Only in RI would a scrapyard occupy such a prime location, protected by the right amount of political contributions to prevent any attempts to reclaim the area.

A tall crane overshadowed two large piles of scrap metal and cars destined for the crusher. The property was surrounded by rusty chain links. There was only one way in, through a locked gate guarded by the obligatory junkyard dogs.

New England remained under summer's control. Rising humidity was accompanied by high temperatures. The unbearable weather brought angst to those who lived in these environs, including the man whose constant honking of the car horn was distressing the yard attendant. At a rusty scrap metal yard associated with the mob, what else is new?

About fifty years old, he had no hair on his head. Six feet tall with a neatly trimmed gray beard. Short and dark-skinned, his jowls would have put Richard Nixon to shame.

He looked at Moon with unforgiving eyes. Neatly pressed jeans, a sweatshirt, and black boots completed his attire. He carried a clipboard with him and had a pager clipped to his belt.

"Sorry, we're closed," he said.

Moon got out of his car and said, "It's eleven o'clock in the morning. How can you be closed?"

As he turned and walked away, the man repeated, "Sorry, we're closed."

"Hey, wait, Aldo sent me," Moon pleaded.

"Aldo who?"

"Aldo Capelli, my nephew."

"And what's your name?" the man asked.

"Richard, Richard Capelli, but everyone calls me Moon."

In the midst of tugging at his beard, the man remembered. "Are you the same Moon Capelli who testified against the family?" he wondered aloud.

"The one and only," Moon replied.

"I thought you were dead."

"I get that a lot," Moon said.

Moon had been around long enough to know you don't ask names in this business unless it's volunteered. "Look, pal, I need a car, and I need this one crushed," he said. Calling him pal seemed a safe option.

"You got cash?" Pal asked.

"I've got plenty of cash." While Moon's statement wasn't exactly true, it wasn't necessary for the man to know that.

"And how do I know you're not a cop?" he said.

"Do I look like a fuckin' cop? I'm driving a stolen car, and there's a bounty on my head. You know why I had to go into hiding. So, what's the problem?"

"Maybe the problem is you're a cop, and I'm about to get busted; that's the problem," Pal said sternly.

"If it makes you feel better, I will say it clearly and loudly, 'I AM NOT A COP.' There you go. Now, if you watch *Barney Miller*, then you know I can't arrest you if I say that, right?"

Relieved, Pal said, "Right, yeah, I like that show; that's the one with Dets. Fish and Wojohowitz, funny bastards."

"Listen, if we can do business, let's do it now. If I like the car, I'll come back and talk to you about *Matlock* or *Murder She Wrote* or any show you want, okay?"

The humor was lost on Pal. "Pull up to the crusher at the back of the lot. I have some cars back there that you might be interested in."

The back of the lot was full of cars of all makes and models, all in a different state of disrepair. For a car, it was the last stop on its journey.

Moon got out of his car and looked around for something that would not stick out but was reliable. If he got back into the family, he'd buy a fancy Cadillac.

If you were in the mob, you had to buy an American car. After all, we must support workers in the car industry. It was only fair since the mob took advantage of auto workers' personal vices to fill its coffers, not to mention the money they stole from union pension and health-care funds.

The yard attendant drove up in a golf cart and jumped off as the engine stopped. The rusty and dirty cart, worn down by the weather and hours of driving, would never be allowed on the course at Pebble Beach.

"Moon, I'll sell you a car and crush this one, but you were never here. Understand?"

Moon interrupted, "Look, I'm going to talk to the Old Man. If it goes well, I'm going to get a seat at the table, and I will owe you a favor."

"Okay, okay, then let's get this done," Pal said. "This is the way it is going to be. I get five hundred to crush this piece of shit. It's your job to get everything out of the car, take the plates, and put them in that pile."

"How do I get another car?"

"Start with this row over here on the left." He pointed to a light pole. "The row numbers start here and run all the way to the front. Walk down until you see section seven. You can have one of those cars for a grand. The cars that run have a blue tag on them and the ones with red tags are junk. The keys will be over the visor."

Moon walked down the rows and rows of cars and all manner of appliances and scrap metal. He thought to himself, *Is this a setup? Is there someone waiting to shoot me down?*

Pal might have made a quick call when Moon wasn't looking. When a strong breeze whipped up from Narragansett Bay, it hit him straight in the face, snapping him out of his paranoia.

Section seven had ten cars arranged like toy soldiers in the first row with little separation between them. A green Ford with a blue tag caught his eye. Carefully avoiding the rusted car parked next to it, he eased into the vehicle. It wasn't in his plans to get tetanus.

Moon flipped down the visor, and the keys fell into his lap. When he turned the key, the starter dragged. He tried again, but it made the same "I don't want to start, I don't want to start" sound. The third time wasn't the charm; it was the fifth time when the powerful Ford roared and started. It was like waking a sleeping lion.

Parking the vehicle in the aisle, he pulled it out of the section. After walking around the 1987 Ford Fairlane 500, he jumped back in and drove slowly to the crane.

Pal dropped his Riviera into the crusher, and it became a lump of metal, plastic, and leather. Europe or Asia would then receive it on a container ship. The materials were then sorted and recycled into new products, such as car parts, furniture, and clothing. The cycle continued, with the materials eventually making their way back to the United States.

From the pile, Moon grabbed a set of RI plates. Pal tossed him a screwdriver and he was ready to go. After that, he drove to the office and waited for Pal to complete the transaction. He needed to get out of there before his newly acquired chariot ran out of gas. The needle on the fuel gauge was buried against the E.

Pal was wiping his hands furiously with an orange rag so stained with oil and grease you could barely see the orange color.

Pal said, "I see you have found yourself a ride."

"I did. How much?" he asked.

"That one has been here for a while, but it's in reasonable shape," Pal replied.

"A grand for this car? You've got to be kidding," Moon snapped.

A bit of anger rose up from Pal's gut into his throat. "You're damn right. It's a grand. If you get arrested or grabbed by the mob in this car, I'm screwed."

Moon fumbled through his pockets and slapped a wad of hundreds into Pal's hand.

"Here you go, shithead."

As Moon drove away, he snorted in amusement and then blew a kiss to Pal.

41

MOON DRIVES THRU FEDERAL HILL

s Moon drove off the lot, he decided to take a ride down Atwells Ave. to see what had changed since he had last been there. Several roads converged at Kennedy Plaza in the form of a wheel with Atwells as one of the spokes. The avenue bustled with foot traffic, and music filled the air. Moon had almost forgotten how vibrant and alive Federal Hill could be. He smiled as he drove away. Moon felt a wave of nostalgia as he drove through his old neighborhood. The sights and sounds were familiar but also new and exciting. He had forgotten how much he had missed this place, and he vowed to make his return memorable.

He couldn't help but catch glimpses of his past as he drove through the city. Moon rolled down his window. A mixture of cigar smoke and garlic invaded his senses, prompting him to inhale deeply.

Growing up on Federal Hill, the most notable characters were the gangsters, of course. Moon had watched these men who rarely worked yet always had money, expensive clothes, and expensive cars. Moon was drawn to this gangster life, even though he knew that sometimes gangsters disappeared.

Moon had known the risks involved in joining the mob. He had heard the whispers, the rumors, and the undeniable truth that sometimes people went missing, either due to violence between gangsters or getting too involved with criminal activities. Despite the warnings, despite all Moon had gone through, he had chosen to disregard the dangers, nonetheless. The allure of money and power was too strong to resist.

Many years earlier, Billy "Cards" Russo had told Moon: "I have good news and bad news about joining the mob."

Young Moon asked, "Okay, give me the good news first."

"Being able to commit crimes whenever you want is the ultimate high. There's nothing better than having a franchise to commit crime," said Billy.

"What's the bad news?" asked Moon.

"No Blue Cross," Billy said, laughing.

42

MOON FINANCES HIS RETURN TO RHODE ISLAND

Before Moon could approach the new boss, he had a list of tasks to complete. However, he found himself in need of more cash and additional credit cards. Feeling desperate, he contemplated resorting to stealing another wallet to solve his financial troubles.

In the city, Moon knew one location that was always thought to be fertile ground for larceny, the Providence Arcade. At the Arcade, there were no pinball machines, video games, or fluorescent lights, but there were plenty of opportunities to liberate a wallet.

Built in the 1800s, The Providence Arcade is on the National Register of Historic Places. As tour guides would tell schoolchildren: "The Providence Arcade was built in 1828. The architecture is Greek Revival, and the large columns evoke ancient Rome or Greece. It is also the country's first indoor mall."

Granite walls supported the two levels of the Arcade, which occupied an entire city block in the shadow of the city's tallest buildings. It was filled with shops, restaurants, vendors, and offices.

During the day, office workers, businesspeople, and students from nearby Brown and RISD crowded the building. This iconic location was taken over by the locals at night. Moon strolled through the Arcade at about six o'clock. His stomach's growl reminded him he hadn't eaten for the entire day.

The Arcade was busy on both floors, mostly with students carrying backpacks. From College Hill, they came down for a break from the monotony of cafeteria food. On high bar tables set in front of the restaurants, they dined on Chinese, Italian, Spanish, and American cuisine.

On the second level, Moon found two upscale restaurants. His eyes were set on La Cucina, an Italian restaurant. He noticed a well-dressed man in his sixties leaning on the wrought iron railing and watching the first floor's activities. The lower level was filled with the sound of laughter, chatter, and a mix of people, some walking slowly and others at a fast pace.

This was Moon's mark. He wore a blue jacket and a button-down dress shirt with an open collar. Besides wearing khaki pants, he had penny loafers on his bare feet. This guy could be the poster child for the unofficial uniform of Newport, Rhode Island. The sweater tied around his neck completed the outfit.

As Moon made his way through the crowd, many people were waiting for their tables. After bumping the man in the shoulder, Moon apologized. Meanwhile, he gently hip-checked him and removed his wallet. Moon had honed the skill of taking something from someone without them even noticing for so many years now that he could perform it without any effort.

Even though he had had success this time and at the airport, continuing to finance his criminal activities with wallet lifts was dangerous because Moon worked alone. Usually, a partner was trained to take the wallet from him. If he was accused of stealing a wallet, the police would not find anything. If his partner was to be arrested, so be it. It was usually a low-level "wannabe" who would do anything to be associated with a made man.

Upon receiving his bill in a few hours, Mr. Newport would discover that his credit cards and almost a grand in cash had been stolen.

Moon drove onto Route 95 South and got off the interstate in Warwick, near T.F. Green Airport. As he took the exit, he remembered that the airport was physically in Warwick, but every airline called it the Providence airport. He snorted and said aloud, "The Warwick Chamber of Commerce must be pissed."

A pleasant bedroom community, Warwick was a mix of commercial and residential areas with one hospital and what seemed like ten thousand strip malls. While growing up, Moon's clearest memory of Warwick was Rocky Point Park.

Rocky Point was an amusement park and shore dinner hall on one hundred twenty acres adjacent to Narragansett Bay. As a child, he recalled eating clam cakes, red chowder, baked fish, steamers, French fries, corn on the cob, brown bread, and watermelon at Shore Dinner Hall. The family saved for weeks to eat at the hall.

Whenever Moon and his brother finished eating, they would beg their parents to take them to the amusement park with its rides, bright lights, and game booths. When they said no, Moon would tell them: "Bringing us down here and not letting us ride on the rides is like taking us to the bakery and not letting us pick out a piece of pastry."

Moon's logic usually didn't win the day, but whenever his father got a cash bonus from the butcher shop, he treated the boys well.

There was something special about those days for Moon. Of course, in those days, he was close to his brother Peter, or Pie, as the neighborhood kids called him. The toughest kid on their block, Charlie Discoli, called the shots. "We're gonna call your kid brother Moon because his face is as round as a pizza, and you're gonna be Pie, get it?" he told Moon's brother Peter one day.

Peter and Moon had no choice but to accept nicknames. In disagreements or fights with each other, they used their real names, but in joking and laughing, they called each other Moon and Pie.

The joy of those moments had long since passed.

Moon wished they could go back to those days, but becoming an informant caused a schism between the brothers that could never be breached unless Moon could find that elusive way to try to earn back his brother's respect.

Driving down Post Road, Moon was still daydreaming about his youth when he reached the Warwick Mall. High-end clothing stores dominated the retail space, but you could also find jewelry, furniture, hairdressers, and a food court where you could take a break after a long day of shopping.

Moon entered the mall and walked around to several stores buying clothes, shoes, and socks. He bought underwear and hoped that it did, in fact, "make him feel glad all under" as promised in the Haines commercial. On his way out, he stopped at Sears and charged two expensive circular saws which he would return in a few hours for a cash refund.

After that, he paid cash for his room at a Quality Inn near the airport. He realized he hadn't eaten all day, so he drove into neighboring Cranston and bought three New York System wiener dogs and fries doused with malt vinegar.

In addition to a soggy bun, the wiener had secret meat sauce, onions, and celery salt. It was easy to sit in the restaurant for hours watching the cash register man holler out, "Six all the way." A shorthand way of saying six wieners with mustard, onion, celery salt, and meat sauce.

Watching the short order cook place the hot dogs in a soggy bun was the real show. The cook, starting at the inside of his wrist and moving up his arm past the elbow, placed each dog with precision and balance.

Next, he slathered the meat sauce and mustard on with a long, thin wooden spoon. He added celery salt from a tin shaker. If you were lucky, he wore a plastic cover over his arm, but most did not. The sweat and hair may have improved the taste, who knows?

A coffee cabinet, Rhode Island's version of a frappé, washed down Moon's meal. Spice, salt, and a warm meat sauce accompanied every bite. Each time he took a bite and swallowed, Moon celebrated his recovered Rhode Island identity.

43

GINO'S YOUTH

New England typically has two seasons: winter and summer. Summer is short and begins in July, with heat and humidity that make breathing an exercise for survival. Gino woke up on Sunday at 7:00 a.m., but there was no hurry since he had the day off. Sometimes, the schedule could be kind and give you a weekend off, though it was uncommon.

Renée had all the air conditioners going at full blast to combat the unpleasant temperature. As she slept peacefully, Gino decided to get up and make coffee. He crept out of bed and quietly made his way to the kitchen. He carefully poured cold, crystal-clear water into the stainless steel pot, the droplets creating a soothing melody as they hit the bottom. With a gentle twist, he opened the lid of the coffee grinder and inhaled the earthy aroma of the beans he had ground the previous night, not wanting to disturb her peaceful slumber. As the aroma of freshly brewed coffee filled the air, he took a slow sip, feeling the warmth and richness of the liquid awakening his senses and setting the perfect tone for the day ahead.

As a child, Gino lived on the second floor of a tenement house without air conditioning. In the summer, waking up feeling like a wet dishrag was nothing new. The heat was oppressive. He would often sit on the fire escape and catch a little bit of a breeze. The family was poor, and there was no money for an air conditioner; all they had was a couple of fans that succeeded in moving the hot air around the apartment. It wasn't simply the heat that kept him up but the mosquitoes. He found solace in dreaming about a life with air conditioning.

As a child, young Gino wondered what mosquitoes were good for in the first place and what purpose they served in Mother Nature. In school, he heard everything about bees and birds pollinating flowers so we could enjoy more beautiful flowers.

Of course, in fifth grade, this science-based theory was not exactly understood. One of Gino's classmates raised his hand and asked, "I'm going to have a new brother or sister. Does that mean Dad pollinated Mom?"

The only real relief from the heat in those days came from the Almagno City pool. Built in the 1950s, it was situated at the base of Neutaconkanut Hill, a pristine eighty-eight-acre area owned by the City of Providence.

During its heyday, it had a ski jump, a large pond for skating and hockey, and a number of trails that revealed streams of crystal clear water, New England stone walls, and walking trails.

Gino and his friends would spend hours in the pool trying to escape the heat. He learned to swim in the summer and ride his sled down the abandoned ski slope in the winter.

On one of those trails, a young girl reported seeing a figure wearing white rags from top to bottom. Because she was so scared, she tumbled down the hill and landed near the basketball courts. The legend of the "Mummy" was born that day. The topic was discussed at school, at home, or on the street corners where young men gathered. They believed an Egyptian king buried under Neutaconkanut Hill wandered out of his tomb in the late hours of the night.

Some suspected that the rumor was started by parents who did not want their children roaming around the woods. Others thought it was a prank, but most youngsters believed, with heart and soul, the mummy was real.

44

GINO BRINGS RENÉE TO THE BEACH
A Year Ago

Gino and Renée enjoyed cinnamon raisin and apple poppy bagels with their coffee this Sunday morning. They savored each bite, smiling as they shared them in their Sunday morning peace. Each time Gino broke off a piece of his cinnamon raisin and handed it to Renée with a smile, she would do the same with her apple poppy.

Renée tuned her Magnavox combination AM/FM cassette player to WPRO. Every Sunday, the station aired a prerecorded interview. Local figures and upcoming events constituted most of the programming. Today, the chairman of the St. Joseph's parade and feast was being interviewed. The chairman expressed gratitude for all the volunteers who help every year and invited the entire community to celebrate with the Italian-American community. As he concluded, he thanked the interviewer and the station for giving him the opportunity to share his message.

"Gino, remember we went last year, and it was great. All the shops were decorated with Italian flags, banners of St. Joseph, and food carts were everywhere."

Gino smiled, "I remember eating at Casa de Roma and drinking that fine red."

While wiping up a bit of cream cheese from her cheek, Renée said, "The religious procession from the Holy Ghost Church gave me a chill. The smell of incense seemed to calm me."

Gino sipped his coffee and remembered, "When I was a kid, the feast was just as important as Christmas." He smiled to himself, remembering how Federal Hill would come alive with accordions playing and people dancing in the streets.

Renée laughed, "I enjoy hearing about your family and the neighborhood. My family stories are boring. We rarely get together other than holidays, weddings, or funerals."

Gino smiled, "It was a lot of fun. We were always running around, playing games, and getting into mischief. We had a big extended family, so there was never a shortage of people to hang out with. What else do you want to know?"

"I want to know as much about you as possible. By knowing about your family, I learn more about you. In some small way, it will help me love you more."

Gino jokes, "You couldn't conceivably love me more. If you did, you would have spared me from meeting your parents."

Renée gave him a gentle slap.

"I'm being serious, Gino, tell me everything, starting with Sundays. You told me it was a big deal for your family."

"It still is. You'll find out when I take you to the beach Sunday. But okay, let me see . . . Sundays always started with me and Mom going to Mass at Holy Ghost Church. The walk from our apartment on America Street took about ten minutes. My mom had already begun preparing the tomato sauce, which we called gravy."

"Did your dad go to Mass?" Renée asked.

"Truthfully, my dad wasn't a big fan of the church and was just as happy to skip it. He packed our old Oldsmobile with beach chairs, a large blanket, towels, and an ice cooler full of food and drinks. After church, we would change into our bathing suits, pile into our car, and head south. Dad would buy ice from the Ice House on Post Road in Warwick.

"I loved watching him hack the large block into submission with an ice pick. As soon as the chunks were uniformly distributed in the cooler, he would snap the lid shut and off we went. I always brought my wiffle ball and bat because my cousins and I loved to play baseball.

"The family then took a long ride down Route 1, hugging the west side of the Bay as it led out of the city. By the time we arrived around eleven, most of the family had already arrived and parked in their favorite spot."

Gino recalled that in his youth, Narragansett lacked a state beach. Near the ocean, there were two private beaches. The owners of Olivo's and Lido's charged a nominal fee for parking on the grass that stretched from the road to the beach. On a busy day, hundreds of cars would be parked in both lots.

Gino continued, "After my dad paid to park, he drove across the grass lot and made his way to a large abandoned and shuttered barn."

"A barn at the beach?" Renée asked.

"I know it sounds weird, but this is where our Cavallaro tribe started meeting every summer weekend since my grandparents passed away. I really don't know how we ended up there."

Gino explained to Renée that the Cavallaro family headquarters was located at the front of the shuttered barn. Families parked their cars in a U-shape in front of the doors. His dad referred to the gathering place as "the Kennedy compound without the money."

"Mom and her four brothers are proud of having been born in the United States. As the youngest and only girl in the clan, Mom was spoiled by her brothers."

Renée interrupted him. "Are you admitting that your mother was spoiled? I'd like to hear you tell her that!"

Gino said, "Seriously, do I look that stupid? You said you wanted to know more about me and my family. I'm just reporting the facts."

They both laughed.

Gino continued, "As soon as the matches were struck, the grills would ignite with a loud pop. On one grill, coffee would percolate. That sound and smell announced the feast was about to begin.

"Oh, then my cousins and I were required to seek out all our aunts and uncles for hugs and kisses when we arrived. The dreaded pinch and twist of my check awaited me as I approached Aunt Pat. In addition to twisting our cheeks, she would scream, *'Sei così carino!'*

"My mother said it meant I was cute. I understood, but why did it hurt so much? She loves you, Gino, my mother would tell me, and those things are part of our heritage."

"So if I pinch your cheeks that means I love you?" Renée chortled.

"Oh, boy. I can't wait. But be careful," Gino said. "You never know where that might lead."

Renée blushed just a little.

She was then told that breakfast consisted of coffee, cheese, cornetti, and sliced meat. For the kids, milk and cereal. Gino had twenty-eight relatives in total. For the clan, two tables were set up: one for the adults and one for the children. "It's like purgatory," Gino explained, "until you get the nod from the adults to join them."

Gino explained that the kids could go to the beach two hours after breakfast but only after two hours. The time was closely checked by Uncle Gaetano, who served in the Navy during the war. All things related to water were under his control. The two hours supposedly prevented stomach cramps.

"They led us to believe that if you got a cramp, you would disappear under knee-high water and be dragged out to sea because you ate two bowls of Frosted Flakes an hour and fifty-nine minutes earlier."

Gino noticed that Renée took great interest in his stories as she smiled and nodded. He continued, "Once in the water, my cousins and I rode the waves to shore like human surfboards. If the waves were high, and if you were lucky, they would toss you around like clothes in a dryer. When you reached the shore, you emptied your bathing suit of sand and ran back into the water."

"Food, food, food. Tell me more about the food," Renée pleaded.

"Okay, okay, slow down," he laughed. "Lunch was pasta, meatballs, salad, stuffed artichokes, and Italian bread. Lots of wine for the adults and crates of assorted flavors of soda for the kids."

"Tell me more, tell me more, tell me more," Renée squealed.

"All right, Olivia Newton-John. Around four in the afternoon, everyone returned to the barn for hot dogs, hamburgers, and sweet Italian sausage. As the family ate, the sounds of Italian and English were interrupted only by laughter. I didn't quite understand everything being said, but my mom had taught me enough to understand my family."

"What about your dad?" Renée asked.

"He didn't even try to learn. I think he liked not knowing what they were talking about. He was able to walk away for some peace and quiet."

. . .

Gino had only ever invited two women to the family beach day: Michelle, and on this Sunday, Renée. They'd been dating and living together for over a year, and this was the first time he had the chance to introduce Renée to his family.

How the day would progress when Renée and Teresa were together was anyone's guess.

Teresa Pompigna Peterson hadn't warmed up to Renée. When they were together, Teresa was a bit cold. Teresa stood just under five feet tall and weighed 105 pounds. Gino compared her to Sophia Loren because of her delicate and proud features.

Her style of dressing was always complimented when she was a young girl. In an awkward manner, she would dip her chin and say thank you, or you're so kind. In her late sixties, she was aging as gracefully as Sophia Loren, but the lines around her eyes and mouth reflected the sacrifices she had made.

Her only son, with whom she found little fault, was the object of her fierce loyalty. Her incredible resilience allowed her to raise him all by herself, even after losing her husband. Despite her hardships, she never wavered in her loyalty and devotion to her son, doing everything in her power to give him the best life possible. For instance, she worked extra hours in the bakery to provide for him. She took him to all his activities and made sure he got the right education.

For her and her son's sake, she never considered remarrying. Her marriage to Albert was eternal in her mind, regardless of how long it lasted on earth. Today, she wore a black one-piece bathing suit. A black-and-white checkered handkerchief covered her head. She wore large, oversized oval sunglasses. As he and Renée approached, she was eating the contents of a cracked walnut.

"Hey, Mom, how are you?" he asked.

"Fine, Gino, fine, and you?"

Before he could reply, Renée said, "Hello, Teresa."

"Hello, Renée, welcome, welcome. Make sure you get something to eat." Teresa's words were polite but not warm.

"Oh, I certainly will. Gino told me all about the food. Can't wait."

"Gino, take Renée to your family, then come back when you have a minute," Teresa said.

With each introduction came a hug and kiss on the cheeks, and everyone was imploring Renée to eat. Renée's head was spinning.

As Renée talked with Gino's cousin, Joy, Gino slipped away to speak with his mother. Now, she was peeling a tangerine on the plastic folding table near her chair.

As Gino approached, he downed a Vicodin with a sip of coffee. He needed the caffeine fix and a dose of courage for what he sensed was about to come his way.

"You wanted to talk, but before you do, can I say something because I know this is about Renée, right?" Gino asked.

"Actually, I want to discuss your future," Teresa said.

"Is there a reason why you treat Renée the way you do?"

"I don't think I treat her any differently than I did Michelle."

"Mom, when we come over, I never see you ask her to help you cook. You always did that with Michelle. Every time she came over you were in your glory. Hovering over her like she was your daughter."

"Gino, you seem to forget that Renée didn't even show up the first time we were supposed to meet. We waited and waited, but Renée was nowhere to be found. I found that disrespectful." Teresa's volume rose a bit. "And she never apologized. You did it for her."

"Come on, Mom, that was when we started dating. I can't remember what happened, but I'm sure it wasn't intentional." Gino tried to convince himself of that, but he knew when Renée had blown off the meeting, she had gone out with some friends instead.

She and Gino had argued about it, and Renée told him she wasn't ready to meet his family. Renée knew that Teresa and Michelle had grown close, and she just wasn't ready to deal with that baggage, especially so early in their relationship.

Teresa calmed down a bit. "Today is a day for enjoying family, so let's not argue. Does that sound okay to you?"

Gino appreciated the truce. "As the saying has it, mother knows best."

"Agreed, my son. Now relax and enjoy your family. Renée and I will be just fine."

While his family entertained Renée, Gino decided to walk down to the beach. Walking across the sand, he spotted his cousins. Amid the blankets and umbrellas, kids screamed and ran from the family to the ocean. For Gino, it brought back wonderful memories, and he hoped to one day bring his own children to this family gathering.

Greeting the clan, he gratefully accepted his cousin Kenny's offer of a beer. Kenny worked as a haberdasher at one of Providence's most prestigious clothiers.

"How's life treating you?" Gino asked.

"My dear cousin, Gino. Today is a beautiful day. I'm surrounded by my family and a lot of food and alcohol. Is there anything more a man could ask for?"

Gino clinked his beer with Kenny's. "Not much, I guess."

"What brought you down today? We haven't seen much of you lately," Kenny said.

"Cuz, with my schedule, I hardly ever get a Sunday off, but today I am, so I thought I'd bring Renée down to meet the family."

Kenny choked a bit on his beer. "Renée? I thought you were seeing your boss, Michelle?"

"Sorry, I thought you knew. It ended after we got jammed up at work."

"Well, you could have fooled me," Kenny said as he gestured behind him with his head.

"What the hell are you doing, Kenny? You look like an ostrich with a stiff neck."

"Look behind me and tell me what you see."

Michelle was lying in the sun a few blankets away from Kenny's family.

"Damn," whispered Gino.

45

HEIR TO THE THRONE

Louie Raimondi was Pasquale Raimondi's only child. When his parents separated, he was ten years old. When the marriage ended, both parents agreed that "the life" was not what their son needed. Louie lived with his mother in a brick colonial house in Mt. Pleasant. But Atwells Avenue is only ten minutes away from this quiet residential neighborhood.

Despite attending Catholic elementary and high schools, young Raimondi did not embrace the Christian lifestyle and often got into trouble. As a spiteful and mean boy, he easily flew off the handle in a flash. He was constantly getting into fights. When he wasn't fighting, he was bullying and stealing.

Every time he got into trouble, whispers and talk erupted.

"Don't you know who his father is?"

"That's the Old Man's kid. Are you sure you want to call the cops?"

"Are you crazy? Not very safe for your health!"

It was the Old Man's dream for his son to be accepted at West Point. He had everything figured out. To be considered for one of the service academies, a candidate typically requires a recommendation from a member of Congress. However, in the case of Rhode Island, none of its two senators or two congressmen were willing to risk their political careers by nominating the son of the head of organized crime in New England. One Southern military school, however, was allocated two slots to West Point for its top two cadets without the need for a congressional nomination.

After a series of less-than-stellar academic results and the hellraising, his son Louie's chances of getting into a military prep school were as slim as Cher giving up her wigs. Faced with this reality, the Old Man gave up his dream.

After that, Pasquale called the admission officer at Rhode Island University, a gambler who owed money to the mob. Upon forgiving his debt, Louie was miraculously admitted to the university. Within two weeks of his admission, however, campus police arrested him for drunk driving and assaulting an officer. He was thrown out before the end of September.

Louie returned home and was summoned to his father's office. It was a hot summer day, and he was dressed in blue jeans and a NY Giants T-shirt. He walked past two of his dad's bodyguards and entered Pasquale's Religious Goods.

Louie walked past the counters and shelves overflowing with crucifixes, rosary beads, pictures of saints, and clothing for priests. The irony was not lost on Louie.

One of the Old Man's childhood buddies manned the store and stood in his usual place near the cash register. Just below, out of sight, a sawed-off shotgun stood at the ready. Louie walked to the back of the store and drew the curtain separating the store from Pasquale's office.

His old man was playing solitaire at a card table. He was dressed in an expensive dark suit, white shirt, and black tie even on this humid day, yet there wasn't a drop of sweat dripping from his brow. Only a grumbling ceiling fan provided cooling.

The father's right foot beat out a rhythm on the floor; his highly polished Italian loafers clicked with each beat.

"Sit down, son; we need to talk."

Louie stared into two pools of darkness that served as his father's eyes. There were bulging veins in his large hands that were gnarled by arthritis. Louie would never admit it, but his dad scared the shit out of him.

"What's up, Dad?"

Pasquale dropped his cards and slowly turned toward his son. "It's time to talk about your future."

Unable to control his cockiness, Louie said, "I don't think I need any career advice. I can make it on my own."

"Son, I love you, but the only career you have ahead of you is as an inmate."

Louie tried to interrupt, "Dad—"

"If you interrupt me again, I'm liable to forget you're my son, capisce?"

Louie lowered his head and stared at the floor. His legs twitched, and his eyes blinked furiously. Sweat collected on his forehead, but the old man remained dry as toast.

"If you are determined to be a gangster, you are gonna have to earn the respect of the real gangsters like the two out front. Guys like that help me put food in your belly.

"In order to rule, you must be feared and respected. Now, some people might fear you because of your name."

The old man's eyes seemed to grow impossibly darker, and his voice more sinister. "But now, no one respects you."

Louie didn't know how to answer. This was a wake-up call, and he better answer the bell or be counted out.

"What do you want me to do?"

"Tomorrow, you will meet Tommy Cabralli at the social club on Acorn Street. Hopefully, he can teach you about this life of ours. Someday, you may become the boss of this family, but you won't survive unless you learn that being a boss can end quickly if you screw up. Leave now."

The old man went back to his game, and Louie knew better than to say or do anything other than to depart quickly.

46

THE ABC'S OF BEING A GANGSTER

Tommy was five years older than Louie, a good soldier and earner in the boss's eyes. He was also a larger-than-life figure, standing at six feet four inches tall and sporting a pug nose and hazel eyes. His height earned him the nickname "Too Tall." To tame his curly hair, he slicked it down with hair gel. He didn't drink, smoke, or gamble like most mobsters. Too Tall returned home to his wife every night. Tommy was both a mobster and a family man. He was a loyal soldier for the boss, earning him a favor, but he also had a life outside of his mob connections. He was married, had a young son, and was a regular churchgoer.

Despite Tommy's personal life, he was a fearless and cold-hearted criminal. He was able to separate his two lives and was unafraid of the consequences of his actions. Louie committed a variety of crimes under Tommy's guidance. While participating in criminal activities together, Louie gained valuable insights and knowledge. Louie began to understand the inner workings of the criminal world. These lessons were invaluable and would enable Louie to become a successful mobster.

Breaking and entering: "Whatever you steal, you take to the Old Man's fence."

Drugs: "Your dad won't let anyone deal drugs. We can protect loads for dealers, but dealing is a death sentence."

Extortion and loan sharking: "A civilian or a business owes you money, and they get behind, you don't kill 'em, you beat them. If they're dead, they can't pay."

Skimming: "Never short the Old Man. He gets 10 percent of everything you earn. If he asks for more, you give it to him. If he catches you stealing, you'll die."

Gambling: "If you want to take over a gambling operation, you need to make sure it isn't protected by a capo or a made man."

Within five years, Tommy had turned Louie into an earner for the family. In fact, Louie learned all the lessons except controlling his anger.

You had to commit murder to become a made man, the mob's equivalent of being granted a franchise, and Louie was no exception. It was called making your bones. In the Silver Lake section of the city, there were two renegade bookmakers who refused to pay the Old Man the standard rate of 10 percent of profits. Tommy was assigned to carry out the hit, while Louie was tasked with driving the getaway car.

Pannone's Market was a small grocery store on Pocasset Ave. It took up half of the front end of a one-story building. The floors were so old they creaked when you walked on them. They sold canned goods, cigarettes, and fireworks in the back room around the 4th of July. Tommy walked in, and when he was done, blood and brain matter covered the floor. Renegade bookies lay dead, victims of greed.

Tommy then summoned Louie into the store, handed him a revolver, and ordered him to put two bullets in each of the bookies.

"OK, kid, you just made your bones because you are as guilty of these murders as I am. Now, let's get the hell out of here."

As a result of the murders, the public and politicians called for an end to mob violence. There was a lot of pressure put on Pascale's operations by the police. Having a fear for his son and Tommy, he sent them to NYC to be hidden and protected by the Colombo crime family.

The Colombo family protected Tommy and Louie until the heat died down. They provided them with false identities and phony identification under the names of "John LaSalle" and "Paul Williams." Tommy and Louie adapted to their aliases quickly and were able to seamlessly blend into society. After three years, witnesses suddenly lost memory of the event. There was no prosecution, and the whole incident was forgotten. As a result, Tommy and Louie were able to return home.

Louie had proven himself worthy and had earned the respect of his father and the New England family. With his newfound reputation, his ascension to the Raimondi family throne was assured.

47

MICHELLE AND SAM OF THE LAKE

As Michelle walked into her duplex, she craved the warmth of a shower to wash away the sand from the beach and the emotions she was experiencing. She was jealous of all the happy couples she had seen during the day. She thought of Gino at the beach as she let the hot water cascade down her body.

Before she could get into the shower, she noticed her answering machine was blinking. In the message, she heard a familiar voice.

"Miss Michelle, Sam here. Can you stop by and see me? I'll be here all day. You know where I am." Michelle smiled and began planning the trip. Sam must have something important to tell her.

Silent Sam, as her father called him, was a gangster now well into his eighties. It seemed that he knew everything that was happening even though he had no direct involvement with the mob.

In the early forties, Sam provided her dad with information about a break-in and robbery at a restaurant on North Main Street in Providence. At the time, her dad was partnered with young detective Walter Smith.

It was December, and Rhode Island was in a deep freeze as they waited inside the restaurant. As they hid behind the counters, and shotguns at the ready, they hoped the information was correct and this was not a wasted overnight stakeout.

They heard breaking glass at 3:00 a.m. They gripped their Remington shotguns tightly and pumped rounds into the chamber.

Walt held up three fingers, followed by two, and then one. A hail of slugs and buckshot stopped the two robbers in their tracks. Just before the first shot was fired, Walt screamed, "Merry Christmas, motherfuckers!"

They fired until their shotguns ran out of shells. Two men with nylon stockings pulled over their faces lay on the floor of the restaurant. The faces of two mob associates were revealed when Ted removed the stockings.

It was the 1940s, just after the era of Bonnie and Clyde, when cops and robbers were constantly engaged in gun battles. No internal investigation occurred, no attorney general reviewed the case, and the media only praised and glorified Ted and Walter.

48

SAM SINGS LIKE A BIRD

ichelle knew she could believe the old man, what-ever he had to say. A visit to his nursing home was a small price to pay. She admired him for surviving the mob for all those years. Her father told her one story about Sam that proved his worth as an informant. In his youth, Sam competed with the two robbers her dad shot to become a made man. After the robbery, Sam had eliminated the competition.

Certainly, that kind of information was worth listening to, and a big arrest would almost certainly catapult her back into the Intelligence Unit. She was determined to make a loud splash and prove she belonged back there. She knew with the right information, it could happen. Every case was like a puzzle she had to solve—every clue was a piece that fit together to reveal the big picture. She was determined to find all the right pieces and put them together to make an arrest.

The nursing home, located in Smithfield, RI, was on a hill overlooking a tranquil lake. As she approached, Sam was sitting on a bench looking out over the lake. He wore silk pajamas and a fluffy bathrobe. A Parodi cigar hung from his lips. It was a small cigar made for Italian immigrants who longed for the taste of the cigars they smoked in southern Italy. While to them, it may have felt like home, to most people, the smoke produced the unpleasant odor of burning garbage.

Sam heard the car door slam. As soon as he saw Michelle, he turned his head and snuffed out the cigar with his cashmere slipper. She wore stretch pants, a sweatshirt, and running shoes. Michelle had just returned from the gym. Damn, she looks pretty, he thought. Laughing to himself, he wished he had been younger.

Sam's slow rise was noticeable. "Michelle, how are you? Thank you for stopping by. By the time you reach my age, all your friends and relatives will be dead."

"Hello, Samuel. You look terrific. Still chasing all the women around the nursing home?"

Sam smiled and gently patted her thigh. "I am, Michelle, but I am too old to catch any of them. Even if I did, I think I forgot what I'm supposed to do."

Michelle was glad they were meeting outside. She could only think of a nursing home as God's waiting room. When she walked down the corridors, she felt the fear and dread of finding herself there one day, probably alone.

Sam leaned in. "Michelle, I know that things have not worked out well for you at work. Your father always treated me with respect, and I never forgot it. It's a dirty business. I survived by working with your father. I never gave up anyone who wasn't a threat to me."

Sam looked down at his feet and saw the crushed Parodi staring back at him. He couldn't wait to light up the next one. "I've kept this secret for many years, but I'm going to share it with you because I'm dying," he said.

Michelle gasped, "What?"

He lifted his head, showing no tears, only a look of resignation. "I have stage four pancreatic cancer, but it's okay. I'm ready. I hope that what I tell you will help you in your career, and in some way, thank your father for protecting me all those years."

Still stunned by his revelation, Michelle said, "Okay. I understand."

"As a young man, Lou had a beef with Gino's father, Albert, over his wife. The beef was settled by Nick Bianco, the capo at the time. Lou never accepted that. After a few months, Albert drives off the road, hits a pole, and dies. Police said it was an accident, but it wasn't."

"Sam, are you saying it was Lou Raimondi, the Don of the family?" Michelle asked.

Taking a fresh Parodi out of his robe, Sam grabbed a gold-plated lighter from the other pocket and looked at Michelle. "Yes, and there is evidence out there that proves it; I can't tell you what it is, but as sure as I am dying, if you dig hard enough, you will find it."

When he fired up the second Parodi, Michelle knew it was time to leave. Getting up, she avoided the first big puff. "Thanks, Sam, thanks a lot." He turned back to the lake through a fog of smoke.

She returned home after experiencing Sam's company and Waterman Lake's scenic beauty. She absorbed Sam's information and tried to figure out what to do with it.

But why am I going to do this now, she thought to herself. She loved Gino passionately and blamed him for walking away, but what happened? Hadn't she walked away also because it was too tough to stick it out and try to save her career?

Michelle knew that this breakup wasn't about the job; it was about how they devoted their passion and intensity to the job, so there was little left for the relationship. I'm such a fool, she thought to herself. I could have made it work. I know that nothing was more devastating to Gino than losing his dad. He never had any closure, never able to move on, and I can give that to him by solving the mystery of his father's death.

She decided to take on the case herself and started to think of ways she could gather evidence and investigate. She also wanted to prepare herself mentally and emotionally for the task, and so she changed into comfortable clothing, popped some popcorn, poured herself a glass of wine, and lit a fire. The sun gave up its reign over the skies as the day ended. She sat on the couch and turned on the TV.

Michelle enjoyed cooking shows, especially the *Barefoot Contessa,* which specialized in Italian food. She found the right channel as the Contessa prepared veal alla mama. Gino's mom, Teresa, taught Michelle many of her family recipes. At that time, she was at the height of her romance with Gino, and his mother had taken her in.

The state police and her dad were her only family, as her mom had passed. Through food, music, and laughter, Teresa's small kitchen on Federal Hill made Michelle feel like she had found a new family. Back then, she felt as if she would spend the rest of her life with Gino.

While Gino was a sharp detective, he sometimes put blinders on to hard truths. Michelle couldn't quite understand why he didn't want to investigate his father's death. She sat down and started to think about Gino and his situation. She knew that she had to help him discover the truth, no matter how hard it was. She finished her glass of wine and started to plan her next steps.

Her mind suddenly cleared, and the illogical had suddenly become logical. Naturally, Gino wasn't interested in investigating his father's death. Teresa would be in danger if he did so, and it didn't take a significant leap of faith to believe that.

As with everything about wise guys, the mob always paints families as noble and honorable. But if it suited their needs, they would kill anyone. A civilian might have been off-limits to some people . . . until some knuckle dragger came along trying to make a name for himself. In the end, the only thing that mattered was money. If they could get away with it, the mob didn't care who they hurt or how. They were willing to do whatever it took to make a profit. Michelle had no idea how close to reality this was to become.

It was well after 1:00 a.m. when weariness forced her to bed.

49

A WALK IN THE PARK

Olney Pond is surrounded by over six hundred acres of Lincoln Woods State Park. This refuge just north of Providence offers beaches, picnic areas, and walking trails. Hundreds of people escape the unbearable heat of the cities during the summer to cool off in the ponds and picnic areas there.

Moon had been walking Lincoln Woods every morning at 6:00 a.m. since his nephew suggested it two weeks earlier. The boss's bodyguard ignored him the first time he walked. With a winter hat covering his forehead and sunglasses protecting his eyes from the low winter sun, he thought he looked like all the older people who walked first thing in the morning.

When Moon saw Lou for the first time, he, too, was wearing a heavyweight parka and corduroy pants. Yet, Lou had foregone a hat, and his long hair locks were exposed. He walked with a sense of confidence. Moon could feel his presence even from across the pond.

As he passed the boss, Moon said, "Good morning." He was pleasantly surprised to receive a cheery response but no hint of recognition.

On Friday of the third week of his walks, Moon, bolstered by the Anisette, decided to exchange more than greetings. As he approached the tunnel leading out of the park and to his car, Moon timed Lou's approach. He exhaled, gave the boss a good morning greeting, and walked alongside him, surprised that the boss didn't object.

"Mr. Raimondi, you might not remember me, but I'm Moon Capelli."

"I knew who you were the day you showed up."

Lou's bodyguard suddenly approached and patted him down looking for a wire or a gun. Then he gave the boss the thumbs up.

"What made you know I was back?"

"The owner of the auto salvage yard answers to me. He called as soon as you left."

Moon thought, *He begged me not to tell anyone, but as soon as I left, he dropped a dime. That's not a surprise at all.*

"I thought about whacking you because, after all, you are a rat. Instead, I had the boys check you out. I had one of them hide in the woods with a rifle, so if you pulled a gun, you would be dead before you raised your arm."

Moon was taken back a bit, but it wasn't as if he wasn't expecting it. "I know I was a rat, but you know I was forced into it, and I never testified against anyone."

"You might not have testified, but you made the dominos fall, and Bobo's crew came down in flames."

Moon said, "Boss, I'm not here to hurt you or anyone. I just have one thing to ask. I want back in because I don't want to be looking over my shoulder for the rest of my life. Tell me how to get back in or put me out of my misery." Moon's voice was not pleading but strong and decisive.

"All right, Moon, I've given this a lot of thought since I found out you were back, and this is how I want it to happen. When you get back to your apartment, there's going to be information on someone who's causing me a lot of problems. You make the problem go away, and you're back."

"That's it?"

"That's what I said. That's what you must do if you want back into the family."

Moon left the park, stopped at a liquor store, and bought some Maker's Mark. When he returned to his room, he could see the tape at the bottom of the door was ripped. Someone had been in the apartment. He grabbed a glass off the shelf and blew into it to get the dust out. He poured three fingers of that glorious liquid into the glass and drank it down, reveling in the slow burn as the liquid traveled down his throat to his stomach.

He placed the bottle on his kitchen table and gazed at the large manila envelope. He opened the envelope while teetering on the edge of intoxication.

Tunnel vision robbed him of his peripheral vision, and the rest of his senses deserted him. The words he read as he reclined back into his chair scorched him like the Caribbean sun.

■ ■ ■

"Aldo, it's your uncle," Moon said into his flip phone.

"Hey Uncle, how did you do with the boss? You're calling me, so that's a good sign."

"I'm not so sure," Moon answered.

Moon was leery of phones and wiretaps. "He's got trash that needs to be disposed of."

Confirming for Moon why his nephew was in the mob and not at Harvard, Aldo blurted out, "What the F? Is he planning to make you haul trash?"

The line fell silent, and Moon waited for the proverbial light bulb to turn on. Aldo broke the silence. "Oh, I understand, Unc. Do you need anything from me?" He spoke at a slow pace like a stage actor searching for his next line.

"Meet me back at that bar tonight around seven, okay? I was up early this morning, so I'm going to lay down for a few hours and then meet you there, okay?"

"Ok . . . Unc . . . I . . . will . . . meet . . . you . . . there."

God, Moon thought, no wonder the mob is dying out.

50

RENÉE V. MICHELLE ROUND 1

enée noticed that she hadn't seen Gino in a while and decided to walk down to the beach. As she located his family, she headed toward them, navigating the hot sand and glaring sun. She saw a female form standing near Gino, and her senses immediately heightened. As she got closer, she saw that it was Michelle, and her mood changed like the tide.

Renée scooped Gino's arm under hers as she came up behind him. All three stared at each other on the beach, waiting for someone to speak. There was an awkwardness that permeated the air around them, as if neither knew what to say or how to act in the other's presence.

Renée sensed that Gino's and Michelle's spark was still there. She couldn't put her finger on it, but it was something she felt in her gut. She was surprised to see how they interacted, and she couldn't help but feel a bit jealous. She knew Gino was still in love with Michelle, even if he denied it.

There was silence until Renée broke it. "Hello, Michelle. What brings you here today?"

"Just telling Gino I have weekends off, so I've been exploring different beaches," Michelle said as she looked at Renée.

Renée smiled and asked, "Have you found a favorite spot yet?"

Michelle nodded and said, "I think so. There's a small beach a few miles away that's beautiful. It's near the port of Galilee. You can watch the fishing boats heading out into the Atlantic."

Renée said, "I haven't seen you in a while. I'm sorry about what happened to you and Gino at work." Her voice was tense. The situation became even more tense when Renée's attempt at being sympathetic came in the form of words that flew like knives into walls.

Michelle's eyes turned cold as if they were frozen. "It was tough for a while, but things are improving. In the near future, I plan to rejoin the unit."

"Let's hope Gino is as lucky. I know if hard work has anything to do with it, he'll be back, isn't that right, love?" Renée looked up at Gino.

Gino tried to stop the train. "Renée, we should be heading back to the barn. Time to eat again."

Continuing her attack, Renée said, "Well, I'm glad everything is going well for you. I recall that your father was a trooper, wasn't he? I'm sure being close to Colonel Smith will help."

"Renée, enough!" Gino growled. He never saw this side of her. The fact that she could handle close combat was undeniable.

The trio's words stopped. Their vocal cords screeched to a halt like a car braking to avoid a collision. At that moment, it became apparent to Gino that there was much more going on besides battered careers.

After shaking the sand from her blanket with a bit too much enthusiasm, Michelle walked away. Renée tried to shake Michelle from her thoughts as quickly as Michelle had shaken the sand from her blanket. Easier said than done.

51

BACK INTO THE MOB?

Moon and Aldo met at the bar near the Bradford factory. Aldo strolled in at 7:15, and Moon was already sitting in a booth. A pitcher of beer was waiting for Aldo to arrive. Most of the factory crowd had left after enjoying happy hour.

Tanya Tucker sang "Some Kind of Trouble" on the jukebox as Aldo slid into the booth to greet his uncle. His uncle's face lit up with recognition. They exchanged a hug while the old familiar tune filled the air.

"Ciao, Zio."

"Ciao, Aldo." Moon slid the envelope he found in his apartment in his direction.

"What's that?" Aldo asked.

"That's what I have to do to get back in."

Aldo pinched the clips open, pulled the contents out, and placed them on the table. He looked at a few pictures and a small map with an address circled.

Aldo asked, "Who is this, Zio?"

Moon leaned in toward Aldo. At the same time, he took the pictures and the map and jammed them back into the envelope.

Moon whispered, "That's Michelle Urban. She's a corporal in the state police. She was the supervisor when I flipped and turned myself over to testify."

Aldo poured himself a cup of beer. "Why would the boss want her dead? You can only imagine how much heat that would generate."

"He's afraid she is going to nose around the accident that killed Gino Peterson's dad," Moon said.

"Gino, Teresa's son from the bakery?" asked Aldo.

"That's the one. Last I heard he got tossed out of the OC unit. His only concern when I got to know him was being in that unit. In a way, we're both trying to get back to where we belong. We're both looking for redemption and a second chance to prove ourselves. I have to make up for my past mistakes and show the boss that I've changed."

There was a puzzled look on Aldo's face. "It doesn't have anything to do with the father's accident or with you."

"I know," Moon said.

Aldo sat up straight. "It doesn't make sense. Why would he care about an accident that happened ten to fifteen years ago?"

"My dear nephew, Lou and I did some things when we were both just starting out. Things that I could blow him out of the water with, but I never said anything to the state police about him when I was in custody."

"Why not?" Aldo asked.

"Because he didn't play any part in putting me in jail. Bobo did all that. It doesn't mean I didn't protect myself when it came to Lou."

The waitress approached, and Moon and Aldo looked at the pitcher, which mysteriously was empty.

"Would you like another?" She had asked this question a thousand times before.

"Sure," Aldo replied.

Moon continued after she walked away. "I think it's more than trying to stop the investigation. He wants to put me in a situation where I'm either killed or do a life sentence for killing a cop." The waitress returned with a fresh pitcher, and the conversation stopped.

"Listen, I need you to get me a gun, something small, .38 caliber. I want a revolver. I just don't trust an automatic not to jam."

Aldo pleaded, "Don't take the job. Just get back into the Witness Protection Program. I'm sure they will take you back."

"You don't understand. I don't have a choice. It's not just me who's in danger."

"I'm not going to give you the gun that gets you killed or puts you in prison for the rest of your life, sorry." Aldo drained his beer and stood to leave. He grabbed Moon's neck and kissed the top of his head. "Good luck, Uncle."

As Aldo walked away, Moon started to think about the gun. He went through his options. Steal one, but how and from whom? Buy one on the street, but there was no one that he trusted.

There was, however, one person he could approach who could get him what he needed.

52

TOOLS OF THE TRADE
Fall 1989

The next morning, Moon poured water into Mr. Coffee at 5:00 a.m. While he waited, he read the morning paper. In the trivia section, he learned Admiral Josephus "Joe" Daniels prohibited alcohol on Navy ships. The term "Cup of Joe" was coined because caffeine had to replace booze.

At the same time, Gino, one city away, waited for his Mr. Coffee to percolate. Both the filter and coffee were put in the previous night before going to bed. Gino was reading the same paper and reading the same trivia question as Moon. They were both also concentrating on the sports scores and racing results.

What began as a strained relationship with Gino evolved into a friendship through their discussions of trivia from the newspaper. Each morning, they would attempt to answer the trivia questions in the paper. Moon excelled at questions involving numbers or sports, while Gino's strengths lay in history and law. Moon's mind was filled with all the useless trivia they had discussed.

The morning routine created a sense of normalcy and familiarity between Gino and Moon, forming a unique bond. Gino became a friend to Moon, and the trivia questions were a way for them to connect and learn from one another.

Moon put on a pair of jeans. He thought that jeans were the official pants of the state of Rhode Island. Walk through any airport and go to the gate for any flight to Rhode Island, and you will see jeans everywhere. They used to call them blue jeans, now with the introduction of black denim, just jeans. With every sip of coffee, caffeine surged through his system and pushed him to the day's task.

On this fall morning, Moon looked out his window. Each pane was covered in frost. If he held his hand at the bottom pane, he could feel the sting of a cold wave. Moon finished dressing. A flannel shirt and a hooded sweatshirt. Moon yearned for the warmth of Virginia. The image he saw in the mirror wasn't exactly Mafia chic. He saw a fifty-year-old mobster dressed like Paul Bunyan.

He arrived at Lincoln Woods at 5:45 a.m. and parked his car in the beach parking lot. He locked his car, left the keys on his front tire, and began to walk. The trees were devoid of leaves and didn't offer much protection from the chilling winds.

There was a light covering of frost on the path that encircled the pond.

The weather had kept fair-weather walkers away, but not Lou Raimondi. Every step Moon took created a crunching sound in the gravel road. As Lou came up behind Moon, the crunching sound doubled.

"*Buon giorno,* Moon."

"*Buon giorno,* Don Raimondi."

Moon tried to gauge the boss's mood, but it was impossible. Moon's stomach was churning, and he could feel sweat beading up under his arms. "I got your package."

Lou turned toward Moon, "And?"

"I'll take the job, but I need a couple of things."

"What do you need?" Lou asked as they continued to walk.

"I need a gun, something small and not traceable. Revolver, not an automatic."

"Done. It will be put in your apartment today. Is there more?"

"Yes. I want you to know I remember everything we did together coming up. All the shit I took from you when you became a made guy. All the people you fucked on the way up—"

Lou stopped and interrupted Moon, "Shut the fuck up because I remember that you're a rat. You lied to the state police, and they bought your shit. I know you care about your nephew, so tread lightly. If you don't do this, your nephew is going to disappear."

Moon wanted to tell him to go fuck himself but thought better of it.

"Get out of here and go do the job I gave to you." Lou continued walking.

Moon spent the rest of the day driving by Michelle's house, trying to determine the best approach and the best escape. Her house was in Warwick, off Post Road, near the airport.

Michelle's duplex had white vinyl siding, black shutters, and a one-car garage for each apartment. There was a set of hedges leading from the back of her property to the edge of the sidewalk.

Moon thought he'd try to follow her, but given her background, she'd pick up the tail quickly. He settled on watching the house. After a week, Moon found the one constant in Michelle's life. She left her home at 7:00 a.m. every day and headed toward Scituate.

53

MICHELLE INVESTIGATES ALBERT PETERSON'S DEATH

Michelle returned to the evidence room on Monday morning, fueled by her visit with Sam and with an unwavering determination to uncover the truth behind Gino's dad's death. She was resolute in her mission, and nothing was going to stand in her way.

Michelle couldn't ask her supervisors for permission to open an investigation. She knew her new assignment was storing evidence, not gathering it, so she couldn't turn the information over to the Intelligence Unit. It was too vague, and they would have no interest in opening a decades-old case.

The Providence Police Department has jurisdiction because they conducted the initial investigation. They would not be pleased if the state police questioned a case they had ruled an accident.

Michelle decided she had to investigate it alone. When there was sufficient evidence to arrest, she would offer it to the Intelligence Unit. To put a boss in jail for a crime he committed decades ago would require the colonel and others to take notice. She hoped that her past sins would be forgiven and that she could return to the Intelligence Unit.

After five o'clock, Michelle left work. She turned on her radio and listened to a Rascals song. It made her wince and think about Gino. He was a Rascals fanatic. Michelle's first stop was a small restaurant on Providence's East Side.

Ruffles was located at the intersection of Wayland Avenue and Angell Street. She considered it the village square of the East Side, the wealthiest section of the city. Here, brick houses were the norm. As if reaching for the sky, ivy crawled up the sides of each house. Almost like an aura of warmth, each home was inviting and comforting. A sense of security spread across the street as if a shield was protecting each house from danger. Children could be seen playing in the front yards with a sense of freedom that could not be taken away. It was a neighborhood that felt like home.

There were other shops and businesses in the area, and Angell Street, which was the fastest route into the financial center, was always congested. Every day, Brown University students rushed to and from classes here. Angell Street led lawyers to South Main Street, where the RI Superior Court was located. In a city built on seven hills, the courthouse was situated at the bottom of one of them.

Michelle, after finding one of the few parking spots near the restaurant, headed into Ruffles dressed for the bone-chilling winter to meet Providence Police Department Sergeant Andrea Wisnowski.

Black pants with a small cuff at the bottom and a plain white blouse gave her ensemble an elegant appearance. She wore a spotted overcoat with a faux fur collar for warmth rather than elegance. Despite the cold, she wore black heels with wraparound straps.

Michelle opened the door to the restaurant, and as she did, the sound of a small bell caused everyone to look up. She stopped and spotted her friend, Andrea, at the far end of the counter. As she walked toward Andrea, she smiled and waved.

Andrea was wearing a colorful blouse with a large scarf wrapped around her neck. The scarf was pinned to her blouse. Michelle knew the pin wasn't just for fashion. It was as sharp as a razor's edge and served as a weapon if Andrea was overcome by a perp. The pin would be stuck in his ear and driven into his skull.

"Hey, Andrea, you look good."

Andrea smiled, "You don't look so shabby yourself. So how are you? How's Gino?"

Michelle answered quickly "I'm fine. As far as Gino, we're not together anymore. He's living with Renée, the former AG."

"Sorry, I asked Mich. How's work, at least?" Andrea said.

"Since my transfer, I've been staring at evidence boxes all day. I'm so bored and can't help but think of all the things I could do instead of looking through these files. I feel like I'm wasting my time here, and I can't help but feel frustrated and restless."

Andrea looked at Michelle, and before she could continue, Andrea said, "Well, now that you're done with your man, if you ever decide to switch sides, I could fix you up."

Their laughter was contagious. Andrea's tongue clicked, "I couldn't wait to tell you I'm involved with someone. She's the coolest thing that's ever happened to me. We're very happy together."

"Andrea, I'm so happy for you. I would like to know all about her, but first I need your help with a very complicated and old case. I know this is a lot to ask, but I wouldn't have come to you if it wasn't an urgent matter."

Andrea responded, "You need my help with a cold case, no problem. But aren't you assigned to the evidence room?"

"I am, but this is personal, and I'm working on this one off the books. The brass doesn't know what I'm doing."

"Do you think that's wise?" Andrea asked, her eyes narrowing.

"Andrea, when Gino was fifteen, his father died in a car accident. They told his family his dad fell asleep at the wheel. Last week, I got some info that it wasn't an accident, but the handiwork of the mob."

Michelle explained to Andrea that the accident happened on Plainfield Pike at the Providence/Johnston line at the foot of Neutaconkanut Hill. All she wanted was a look at the original case file, to check out the location, and to talk to some people in the neighborhood.

"Michelle, you want me to dig out a case that's at least twenty years old and just hand it over to you?"

"Andrea, you and I know what it took for us to get where we are in this macho 'my dick is bigger than your dick' world. All I'm asking for is a chance to get back to what I lost. To be relevant again."

Andrea took a long sip of her coffee, looked around the restaurant, and said, "I'll get the file for you, but first, you have to admit to me that part of this is about him. It's still on your mind that you and Gino can get back together."

Michelle smiled a bit. "Oh, I don't know . . . right now, I just want to solve the case."

Andrea nodded as if she had never believed anything less. "I'll get the file to you tomorrow."

"Thanks, Andrea." Michelle breathed a sigh of relief. "Now tell me all about this new love of yours."

54

THE PROVIDENCE POLICE
INVESTIGATION

Michelle returned to work the next day. Per usual, she spent her time filing away evidence and recording its location. A small radio set tuned to a local talk show station was her only companion.

At 5:00 p.m., she locked up the evidence room and headed home. On Post Road near her house, Michelle picked up a roast beef sandwich from Walt's Roast Beef.

As she approached her duplex, she glanced at the For Rent sign. A young couple who had been her tenants had bought a house and moved out. She would take the time to carefully select not only tenants but also close neighbors.

Michelle checked her mailbox and collected letters, bills, and junk mail. As she opened the screen door, a file folder fell out. She scooped it up and opened the door.

Michelle dropped the mail and opened it right away. The first thing she saw was the Providence Police accident report.

The report started with standard language. The accident occurred on October 27th, 1967, at 11:45 p.m. The weather was listed as misty with an occasional shower, the roadway was described as an undivided two-lane roadway.

The report continued: Albert Peterson, a single operator, was traveling west on Plainfield Pike (Route 14) when he left the roadway and struck a utility pole. According to the report, the front grill and left side of the vehicle were damaged.

The file held two other documents. An autopsy found that the victim died from blunt force trauma to the chest and head. A dried blood stain was also seen on the victim's shirt, but it was not caused by the crash. The cause of death was determined to be accidental.

A hit-and-run squad detective, Tom Madden, also filed a report. There were no witnesses in the rural area where the car ran off the road. Afterward, he stopped at the intersection near the accident scene to see if anyone could help. Unfortunately, the people living in the area were reluctant to give any information as they were afraid of getting involved. Tom was unable to get any leads or witnesses from the people living in the area.

Three business owners at the intersection of Plainfield Street and Webster Avenue were interviewed by Madden. Neither the owners of Venice Pizza nor Carl's Market had anything to offer. Pete Tabor, the owner of Pete's Spa, recalls Albert stopping in for breakfast late at night after his shift at the mill. He couldn't recall if he did the night of the accident.

Michelle recalled Gino often visiting that store as a child. He described a counter with stools and a few tables. Everything was made to order. Penny candy, magazines, and toiletries were also available. Often, he would take her for a ride through his old neighborhood and was always comforted that the three businesses were still thriving.

The report indicated Sue Tabor or Mrs. Pete, as she was called, kept an eye on all the customers and supervised the cash register. Although Albert would often come for breakfast and buy a copy of the *Evening Bulletin*, Mrs. Pete told Detective Madden she didn't recall him coming on the night of the accident. Michelle was intrigued by the next section of the report.

A well-known fact in the neighborhood is that the race results from Lincoln Downs held the winning combination in the numbers pool. The winning number for the week came out in the late edition of Boston's *Record American*.

Pete's Spa sold out of copies of the paper most times. There was a lot of disappointment as customers flipped to the race results. Sometimes, there was an occasional yell indicating someone had won.

The bookie would take the bet and tell everyone that the win, place, and show numbers before the decimal point for the seventh race at Lincoln Downs was the winner. If a winning horse paid 112.14, the show horse 94.81, and the place horse 62.41, betting 242 was a winner.

Madden guessed that Albert may have stopped in there for the *Record American* shortly before the accident. Madden visited the Spa late at night on four occasions but could find no one who remembered seeing Albert that night.

Michelle didn't find it surprising that no one wanted to be involved at the time. However, one person knew more about that night than most.

55

MICHELLE VISITS TERESA

ichelle woke up to snow falling heavily on the state. As she looked out of her window, she could see that it would be a challenging day for both motorists and troopers dealing with the storm. She got dressed in her green state police snowsuit with gold stenciling. These suits were provided to troopers after the blizzard of '78 to ensure a uniform appearance. Before the blizzard, troopers wore a variety of warm sweaters, gloves, and hats, making it difficult to distinguish them from survivors of an Arctic expedition.

Michelle started her drive to work. On Route 295, a car had spun off the road and was sitting in an area of snow-covered

• 248 •

grass between the northbound and southbound lanes. Michelle stopped, and after finding that the driver was not hurt, she called for a tow truck.

As soon as she arrived at headquarters, the lieutenant ordered her to assist with the storm. During the storm, Michelle was assigned to Route 95 in Providence. The rest of the day was spent assisting motorists and dealing with accidents. Driving on the highway during a snowstorm was incredibly dangerous. The roads were covered in a thick blanket of snow, and visibility was low. Michelle had to be extra careful to avoid any accidents. She worked hard to help anyone who was stuck and was able to help many motorists get back on the road safely.

During snowstorms, many accidents occur as drivers lose control of their vehicles and slide off the road. Michelle came to the aid of two motorists—one who had slid off the entrance ramp and one who had slid off the exit. Both collided with light poles. Her mind immediately turned to Gino's father's fatal accident.

Did Gino's father gamble? Did he owe the mob money? What was he doing on Plainfield Pike the night of the accident?

In the afternoon, the snow dissipated, and by 5:00 p.m., the highways were passable but slushy. Michelle radioed dispatch that she was going off duty and would return home. Her detective car would be waiting for her when she arrived in Scituate the following morning.

◾   ◾   ◾

After taking a quick shower, she dressed, hopped into her Honda Civic, and headed to Federal Hill. There, she picked up half a dozen croissants and two espressos from A Small World Bakery.

Just as the sun began to set, Michelle pulled up to the tenement on America Street. Michelle climbed the two floors, and she gently knocked on the door.

"Who is it?" the soft voice of Teresa Peterson asked.

"Mrs. Peterson, it's me, Michelle Urban."

Teresa smiled and held out her arms when the door opened. "It's been so long, Michelle. I'm so glad you stopped by." Michelle put the coffee and pastries on the table and hugged Teresa tightly.

After releasing Teresa from her hug, Michelle said, "I'm sorry I didn't call you first, but I needed to talk to you."

"It's been too long since we spoke. How are you?"

Michelle was last there with Gino two years ago. Almost nothing had changed. The apartment was neat and tidy, and the room was filled with the aroma of pasta sauce. Pictures of the family adorned a small shelf opposite the sink and electric oven. Oil heat was installed in the kitchen to replace the old kerosene heater. As hot water ran through the pipes, radiators clicked and banged. The room was filled with warmth from the heat and the memories of family and friendship.

Teresa talked about her health, the changing neighborhood, and, of course, her son, Gino. Neither Teresa nor Michelle mentioned Renée, and Michelle wasn't sure if Teresa was being polite or chose not to say anything bad.

Teresa finally sat, drank her espresso, and picked at a croissant.

"What brings you here today, Michelle? Everything okay?"

"Everything's fine, but can I ask you a few questions? You see, I'm looking into Albert's accident."

Suddenly, Teresa's hands trembled, and she put the coffee cup down. In a way, she looked like she was rearing up like a bear protecting its cub as her back stiffened. The raspiness in her voice increased as she spoke.

"You're investigating Albert's accident? Why are you doing that? Why isn't Gino here? I don't understand. Isn't this something he should tell me?"

"Please, Teresa. Calm down. Please. I'll explain everything." Michelle feared this was going off the rails.

"Explain what? We know what happened to him. First, they said it was an accident, and then someone told Gino it was that thug, Bobo Detroia."

"I'm not sure that's what happened, and I think you doubt it too. Isn't that right?"

Teresa became quiet. She almost seemed to fold inward like a spider. "You mean Lou Raimondi?"

"Yes, Lou Raimondi. Please tell me everything."

"I will, but you must promise never to tell Gino any of this. I don't want him to think anything less of his father . . . please."

"I'll try."

Teresa continued, "My Albert was not a terrible man. He worked hard, but he liked to gamble. We would play our numbers every week, placing nickel and dime bets, hoping we'd win. When Albert got out of work on Tuesday, he would check the *Record American* to see if he had won." Her voice cracked a bit, and she took a long sip of coffee before she continued.

"Most waited until Wednesday afternoon to collect their winnings, but if you were in a hurry, you could drive to the Social Club in Olneyville and get paid."

Michelle asked, "Is that what Albert was doing the night he went off the road?"

"I think so, but I don't know for sure."

"I know this must be incredibly difficult, but please tell me about Albert and Lou."

A stiffening sensation spread through her body. "Lou is a pig. He touched me while we were dancing at a party. Gino had just turned one year old, and we were celebrating his birthday. As Albert jumped in, the two almost got into a fight. Then Lou screamed that he thought it was time for me to be with him instead of Albert. I quickly realized that Lou was not the gentleman I thought he was."

In the palm of her hand, she kept a Kleenex to wipe away the gathering tears. "Lou would harass Albert whenever he fell behind on his bets. I remember Albert coming home one day looking like he had been in a fight. He tried to tell me some of the shelving at work fell on him. I didn't believe him, and he finally told me he had gotten into a fight with Lou."

Teresa feared for her family and his safety after what he had done. Michelle decided that she needed more, but she wasn't willing to press Teresa anymore.

Everything pointed to Lou as the likely suspect: he had motive, opportunity, and the means to commit the crime. Michelle knew that if she was going to solve the mystery, it would begin and end with Lou Raimondi.

56

MICHELLE GOES TO THE
ACCIDENT SCENE

After leaving Teresa's apartment, Michelle drove to the accident scene. While driving down Atwells Avenue, she picked up Plainfield Street, which became Plainfield Pike or Route 14. On Route 14, she listened to "Everybody Wants to Rule the World" by Tears for Fears as her Honda Civic traveled west. Leaning back against the headrest, Michelle turned up the volume. The mob wanted to rule the world, and she knew they would not allow anything to prevent their goal. No country, law enforcement agency, rival gang, and certainly not Albert Peterson.

Michelle traveled down Route 14 looking for Narragansett Electric Pole 632 near Neutaconkanut Hill. The Providence Police report indicated that this was where the accident occurred. In the more rural areas of the state, houses and farms were so spread out that the police used pole numbers to find locations.

Michelle parked on the side of the road after finding the pole. She stepped out of the car looking for something that pointed to anything other than an accident. Something she could use to build a case, even after all these years. Desperate for something proving Lou Raimondi or the mob was involved in the crash.

Pole 632 was located about halfway between the basketball courts and the pool on the Neutaconkanut Hill side of the street. Looking toward the ski slope covered in snow and sledders, she turned around. To the right, a baseball diamond, under the glare of large spotlights, on which young kids slid into the snow-covered bases screaming with glee. Parents took photos to capture the joy of youth.

She remembered Gino telling her about the hill. Whenever they drove by, he would point over and tell her the story of the mummy for the thousandth time.

The crash scene did not yield anything of interest to Michelle. The road had been repaved, and the pole replaced many years ago. Although she wasn't expecting much, this was yet another dead end.

57

MICHELLE VISITS HER DAD

Michelle was off duty today since it was Saturday. She always visited her father when she needed direction, and this was certainly one of those times. Michelle relied on her father's law enforcement training. He was always willing to listen and provide sound guidance based on his years of experience.

Retired RISP Lieutenant Ted Urban lived in the Norwegian assisted living apartments in Scituate. His Norwegian heritage had made him think that these apartments would be appropriate for him and his brethren. Soon after, he realized the apartments were owned by a conglomerate whose properties were named after European countries.

The Norwegian apartments were in the village of Hope in the southern section of the town. As far as Rhode Island goes, Scituate was one of the largest towns, but the reservoir took up most of the land mass. In the smallest state in the union, large is relative. Rhode Island students were often told there were ranches in Texas larger than Rhode Island.

On a map, the reservoir looks like a winged bird, possibly Phoenix rising from the ashes. The reservoir effectively divided the town in half. The village of North Scituate is home to houses, the post office, and the RI State Police Headquarters. To the south, Hope Village is home to mills powered by tributaries flowing into the Providence River and Narragansett Bay.

When Michelle arrived at the parking lot of the Norwegian apartments, Bette Midler's "Wind Beneath My Wings" was playing. She took a moment to organize her thoughts and figure out how to explain to her father that she was investigating outside the chain of command. She was certain her father had also worked outside the lines, but she wanted to make sure he knew she had a good reason for doing so herself.

The apartments were two stories high, built using brick that had a fieldstone look. Each apartment had a large pane window and two smaller panes on either side. A crank was used to open the screened-in side windows.

The main entrance was almost constantly busy with drop-offs and pickups. Residents were picked up by vans for shopping sprees, entertainment venues, or a visit to Foxwoods Casino in Connecticut. Residents were often taken to the hospital or doctor by ambulance. This was the scene at a busy assisted living complex, where the elderly residents were cared for and given a safe and stimulating environment. Many of the residents were dependent on the staff for their daily needs and outings.

Michelle parked her car and walked in.

58

FATHER KNOWS BEST

Theodore "Ted" Urban lay back in his armchair, a homemade quilt draped over his legs and waist, providing comfort and warmth. His weary eyes fluttered as he clutched the novel firmly in his hands, the weight of his exhaustion pulling at him. Slowly, the words of the novel began to blur and fade as he succumbed to the pull of slumber. Lost in the world of the book, he was oblivious to the passage of time as he drifted into sleep.

When Michelle walked into the apartment, she decided not to wake him. She looked around and recognized all the furniture. Six months after her mom's death, she and Gino selected what would be delivered to the apartment from the home her mom and dad shared for sixty years.

Three of his retired police friends also lived in the Norwegian apartments, and they would talk endlessly about days gone by. It gave her comfort to know he was among his brothers in arms. In the dining room, everyone talked about their medications, illnesses, and ungrateful children and grandchildren. He would always go there if he could sit with his three buddies. These four old cops would tell tales of their days on the force, the criminals they had arrested, and the detective work they had done. They would share stories of the daring escapes, the funny and sometimes tragic incidents, and the camaraderie they had shared with their fellow officers. It was a time of reminiscing and telling tall tales, and it was a pleasant distraction from the realities of growing old.

Ted's health issues began shortly after his retirement. He suffered from lumbar spinal stenosis, which he blamed on all the running he did to keep in shape. It also made him unsteady on his feet. Two years later, he had his right kidney removed after a small cancerous tumor was found. After that, a bout of skin cancer required a generous amount of tissue to be removed. Each year, he would return to his dermatologist and have the precancerous cells on his face frozen with liquid nitrogen.

He would tell Michelle: "Getting old isn't for sissies."

Ted slowly opened his eyes when he sensed someone in the room. Upon seeing Michelle, his eyes welled with tears, and he smiled. "Hello my beautiful daughter. How are you?"

"I'm fine, Dad. Are you behaving?"

"Well, I'm trying. But there are a lot of pretty young girls here, and I confess to looking."

Michelle gave him her stern look. "Looking is okay, Dad, but no leering, you know what I mean?"

"You mean looking at them constantly, hoping they bend over, especially when cleavage is showing, and asking for the 'head' nurse. All that's no good, huh?"

"Enough, Dad. Just stop. Let's move on, okay?"

He realized she was here for a reason, so he said, "Okay, enough. What's up?"

In the next hour, Michelle told her dad about Gino, Sam, her dad's informant, and her meeting with Teresa.

"Did your boss ask you to investigate the accident?"

"No. This is off book."

"Okay, so did Gino ask you to do it?" Ted asked.

"No, he didn't. The truth is, he would probably be upset if he knew," Michelle said.

With a puzzled look, Ted said, "Why would he be upset if you investigated his father's murder, especially if the killer is still out there?"

"Just before we got tossed out of the Unit, one of the mob's lawyers gave Gino a BS story about how one of the guys Gino just sentenced to life was responsible. Pretty convenient, I'd say, but Gino wants to believe it. Gino is convinced, but I am not. This is too suspicious. Something else is going on, and I'll find out what it is."

Ted was known in his day as a tough son of a bitch. That generation of police officers had to be. That's the way policing was done. At the same time, this was his only daughter who had been through a series of challenges she likely didn't deserve.

He looked at her now as she stared at her shoes, then at the ceiling, finally at the door.

Ted took a deep breath, his voice filled with concern. "Michelle, you're a cop, a good one. Good cops always follow their instincts, and I trust yours. But please, in the meantime, be careful. Don't do anything foolish, okay? Your safety is my top priority."

"Okay, Dad, I promise. I'm going to leave now, but I'll be back."

"I know you will, so keep in touch, okay?"

"You bet, Lieutenant," Michelle said. Then she saluted him, not in a mocking way but as a sign of respect. As soon as he returned the salute, she kissed him, turned on her heels, and left.

59

RENÉE CONFRONTS GINO

Gino looked forward to sleeping as he headed home after working nights. He recalled why such an assignment was called the graveyard shift. In days before medical science, people were sometimes buried alive. Coffins had strings attached to bells on the surface. If you awoke in a coffin, you could ring the bell by pulling on the string. Grave keepers worked during those early morning hours because, in the early morning silence, they could hear their casket bells ringing and could begin digging you up.

Overnight shift survival methods vary from person to person. Each trooper works four ten-hour nights beginning at

10:00 p.m. and ending at 8:00 a.m. Then it's two days off. A few of Gino's friends stayed up until about 2:00 p.m. and slept for four or five hours. Some would go to bed as soon as they got home and sleep for four, five, or even six hours before coming to work.

During the predawn hours, typically between 4:00 and 6:00 a.m., as darkness slowly gives way to light, he struggled to stay awake. It was an epic battle to keep his eyelids open. The ebb and flow of his eyelids reminded him of the Battle of Gettysburg. Gray coats tried to overtake entrenched blue coats in waves, advancing and retreating repeatedly in oppressive heat.

Gino believed the human body was not designed to work overnight. In his mind, it would be like being right-handed and then given a job where you are only allowed to use your left hand.

After a few weeks, Gino discovered what worked for him. He would go to bed as soon as he got home. Before heading home, he usually had breakfast with his shift. Gino would sleep until 5:00 p.m., wake up, shower, shave, and have dinner with Renée before leaving for the barracks.

Usually, Renée spent her mornings teaching, preparing, or attending academic meetings at the college, but today was different.

When he tried to unlock the apartment door, it was already open. He entered and looked toward Renée, who stood near the stove, her arms crossed. Coffee infused the air, but Gino's trepidation overshadowed it.

Renée looked angry. She was wearing a RISD long-sleeve T-shirt paired with black jeans and white Reeboks. The tight bun in her hair made her look fierce.

"Good morning, Renée. Hey, what's up? Is everything okay?"

"Yeah, I just want to talk, okay?"

"Sure. Can I pour a coffee first?" Gino asked.

"I'll do it," Renée said. Gino sat at the table.

Renée poured two cups from the pot and placed them on the table. When she sat down, she opened the bottle of anisette on the table and poured some into her cup before offering it to Gino.

Sensing a change in the atmosphere, Gino said, "I think I'll pass on the coffee and just have the anisette."

Renée asked if it had been a busy shift.

"Not really, slow, which makes it challenging to get through the night. If there are no calls and you want to stop cars, after 2:00 or 3:00 there's really nobody out there on the road."

Renée sipped her coffee. Gino's throat tingled a bit as he swallowed the alcohol.

"Renée, I know something is wrong. Could you tell me what I did?"

Renée reached up onto the kitchen counter, grabbed an envelope, and slid it over.

"What's this?" Gino asked.

"Well, Gino, that's a wedding invitation from my friend Courtney. We were in the same sorority, but she was two years behind me in school."

Gino, oblivious as most men are, said, "Hun, if you don't like her, you don't have to go."

"Seriously, Gino? It's a plus-one invitation, and I guess you are my plus-one. Although I would much prefer it be addressed to Mr. and Mrs. Gino Peterson, I have had no such luck."

Gino was tired, and when he was tired, he became pissy. "Wow! Where's this coming from?"

"It's coming from wanting to be with you for the rest of our lives. It's about having a family. I'm thirty years old, Gino, and my biological clock is ticking. I don't want it to run out while you're playing cop and taking pills. You have no idea what it's like to long for a child. I thought you wanted us to be together and raise kids. I want that for me."

Gino hesitated. "It is what I want, but everything is going so well between us. What's the rush?"

Renée softened a bit. "Gino, we've been together for over five years. I just need to know where this is taking us."

"Where do you want it to lead, Renée?" Gino asked.

"Seriously, Gino? I just told you! For God's sake, I've been invited to my girlfriend's wedding, and we're not even engaged."

The softness was gone, and Gino was facing the steel-nosed prosecutor he remembered.

"Renée, I'm just getting out from under losing Marty and Billy at the courthouse. I'm trying to work my way back into the IU. There are a lot of things happening right now."

"That was four years ago, and I'm not buying it; this is about Michelle. This is about her, isn't it? You're still hung up on her, aren't you?"

"I didn't say that," Gino shot back.

"You didn't have to." Renée got up from the table, finished her coffee, and walked toward the door. "I'm off to work."

Gino was still stunned by Renée's words. He sipped on the anisette aimlessly. While Gino contemplated Renée's words, he had no answers for her. At least not the kind she was seeking.

He went to bed, too tired to think, and hoped everything would be okay when he awoke. He was trying to put off thinking about the consequences of his actions by sleeping, thereby avoiding the reality of the situation. He knew he couldn't delay the inevitable, but he was hoping that when he awoke after a fitful sleep, he'd have the courage to face the situation head-on. He was ready now to accept whatever consequences there might be.

60

RENÉE V. MICHELLE ROUND 2

Most of Renée's time was spent grading papers. At the end of January, midterm grades were due, and that date was rapidly approaching. Students in her criminal law class had to write a case summary of Spinelli v. United States. In this case, the question was whether the information passed from an informant to the FBI was sufficient to show probable cause.

While reading about informants, she recalled meeting Gino for the first time. Her position at the RI Attorney General's office in 1983 was Chief of the Criminal Division. Michelle was called to a meeting with state police representatives. There was an informant who would testify about the mob hit on Richard "Dickie" Calderone.

During her time working with Gino and Michelle, Renée heard rumors about their involvement. Like ships caught in gale winds, she always thought their relationship would crash onto the rocky shore.

Renée graded all the papers and recorded the grades in her green grade book. As she leaned back in her chair, she munched on a pencil and thought about the morning. Renée felt guilty for being so harsh with Gino.

There were so many other ways to approach the subject, but the invitation triggered a sense of loneliness. Renée decided she would make amends by picking up some pastries at Gino's favorite bakery on Federal Hill.

Renée drove to Federal Hill from campus. She listened to B101—the home of your favorite oldies—during the twenty-minute ride. In front of It's a Small World Bakery, she found a parking spot on Atwells Avenue. When Renée crossed the street, she noticed graffiti on the ornately stenciled front window. Somebody had spray painted "BUT I WOULDN'T WANT TO PAINT IT" under the words "It's a Small World."

Renée laughed as she entered the bakery. She took her number and waited. Ten minutes later, she was greeted by a large man wrapped in white and covered in flour. As she contemplated a quick trip to see Teresa, she ordered two cornetti (which she didn't dare call croissants in this store).

Renée left the bakery, crossed the street, put her pastries in the car, and drove to Teresa's apartment. She saw someone leaving the house as she turned off Atwells onto America Street.

The woman wore a Joules rain parka and a rain bucket hat. Blond hair dangled from the hat. Renée watched as the woman drove away in a black sedan. It was Michelle.

61

GINO AND TERESA

Gino was waiting for Renée when she arrived home around 5:30 p.m. Renée held up her hand as Gino began to speak. "First, I apologize for what happened this morning. I brought you some pastries from your favorite bakery."

"Renée, no need to apologize, but let's sit down and talk."

"I'd like to save that discussion for another time. There's something you need to know," Renée said, taking her coat off and setting the pastries down.

Gino's eyebrows twitched rapidly with agitation, but he wisely chose to remain silent. "I also bought your mother a couple of croissants when I bought your pastries. As I drove over there, I saw Michelle coming out of your mother's house. Maybe it was just a social visit. Maybe she just wanted to check on Teresa," Renée said.

Gino replied, "Why the hell would she be going to see her?"

"I don't know, but before you say anything to her, maybe you should check with your mom."

Gino said nothing. He just walked over to the phone and dialed. On the third ring, Teresa answered with a friendly hello.

"Hello, Mom."

"How are you doing, Gino?"

"I'm fine, but I have to ask you if you had a visit from Michelle."

"Yes, she was here."

Gino tried not to sound angry. "Why was she there?"

"Just saying hello, that's all." He could hear a slightly higher pitch to her voice. He knew she was hiding something.

"Mom," Gino said, then took a long pause.

She was losing the strength of her voice. "All right, she asked about your father's car accident. I didn't want you to be upset. I asked her not to say anything to you."

Her pleading now demanded Gino's forgiveness.

"Mom, it's all right. Don't worry, she didn't say anything to me. No need to worry. I'll talk to her."

Teresa asked, "How did you know?"

"Renée was going to see you, and she saw Michelle leaving your apartment."

Teresa muttered something in Italian.

"What, Ma?" Gino asked.

"Nothing. I'm sorry, but I may have said some things that I've never shared with you."

"Like what?"

Teresa gathered her thoughts, "Gino, I have always told you the truth, but I have kept some things from you to protect the memory of your father. I was afraid you would lose respect for your father if you knew of his faults." Gino sensed the unshed tears in Teresa's eyes, noticing the subtle sound of her sniffling. He could almost see her delicate hand reaching for the tissue she always kept tucked up her sleeve.

"After all we've been through, I would never ever lose respect and love for my dad. We all have flaws. Nobody's perfect. He loved us, and that's all that counts."

"Oh, Gino, even though it was difficult, I should have trusted you to handle the truth. It would have been better if I had been honest. I'm sorry."

"It's okay. Time to move forward."

"I love you, Gino. Call or stop by soon, please."

"I love you too, Mom," Gino said as he hung up the phone.

"Well?" Renée asked.

"What am I supposed to do with that?"

62

MOON'S DESCENT INTO HELL

oon took the Smith & Wesson revolver from the nightstand drawer. He carefully removed the .38 caliber rounds, examined them, and then reinserted them. After spinning the chamber, he tucked the gun into his waistband as soon as it clicked into place.

He had dressed by 6:00 a.m. It was still cold, so he put on cords, a hooded pullover, and a knit cap over his newly shaved head.

On the kitchen table, he left a note for Aldo before leaving the apartment. The desire to keep his nephew safe drove him to write slowly and deliberately. His chances of surviving were as low as the temperature in January. If he didn't survive, he made sure his instructions to Aldo were clear, concise, and loving.

The sun was shining, and the weather was cold but comfortable. Although it was still winter, the lack of strong winds significantly reduced the wind chill.

As Moon walked outside to his driveway, he looked through the gray clouds at the rising sun. He took a deep breath, made the sign of the cross, and got into his car. Two days ago, it rained and snowed, resulting in slush covering the streets, but the interstate remained dry.

Listening to radio talk shows was Moon's favorite pastime. Today the callers were bitching and moaning about Rhode Island, which was the norm.

His favorite host was Jack Comely. When Moon turned on the radio, Jack's deep voice usually comforted him, but today it distracted him. The twenty-minute ride seemed to take an hour.

As he arrived at Michelle's house, the sky was filled with thick, ominous clouds, casting a shroud of darkness over the surroundings. Not a single ray of sunlight pierced through the dense overcast sky. Moon drove around the block twice just to be sure there were no cops around.

After parking around the corner, he pulled his knit cap down over his head and neck. His eyes and nose protruded through large holes. Leaving behind the warmth of the car, he walked toward the familiar hedge, his constant companion during his surveillance of Michelle.

With every step, Moon dreaded the crunch of the snow-slush combination. His pants became soaked when he sat down in the shrubs. Immediately, his body felt a chill, but that only lasted for a moment.

What was not going away was the battle raging in his head. From the moment Raimondi gave him the assignment, he struggled with murdering a cop. Moon knew that if he killed a cop, the whole world would turn on him.

Yet, the only nephew he had would die if he didn't act. In many ways, his nephew was like a son. He was willing to make the ultimate sacrifice to save his nephew.

He remembered how proud his brother was when Aldo was born. A son would carry on the family name. What would that name be if a Capelli murdered a police officer? No one could escape that legacy.

A glance at this watch showed 6:45 a.m. It wouldn't be long now before he'd have to decide. Looking at the house, he could see the small bathroom light. He imagined her putting on the finishing touches of her makeup, not knowing what was about to happen.

Another glance at his watch, 6:55 a.m. Moon slid the gun out of his waistband and gripped it tightly. How could I let Raimondi play me like this? Could I save myself by turning myself in?

Moon looked up and Michelle was outside her house locking the door. There was no time to think, only to act.

After locking her front door, Michelle walked down the cobblestones to her cruiser. Her arms were laden down with what looked to be case files.

As she unlocked the car door, she dreaded the fact that she didn't have a remote starter for her car. Her peripheral vision, however, caused her to turn and look. A man wearing dark clothing and a ski mask quickly closed in on her.

Instinctively, she dropped the files and reached for her gun. Michelle flipped off the safety on the Beretta and began to raise it.

The man continued to walk toward her. She saw the small revolver, but he was holding it at his side. Everything happened in an instant. There was no time to think, only to react.

She heard a yell that was primal and desperate, loud and guttural.

They raised their guns and fired at each other. Searing pain erupted in her shoulder. As her Beretta flew out of her hands, she was forced backward.

Getting shot for real is nothing like the movies. There is searing pain, horrific fear, and formidable anger. The body reacts to the physical trauma, trying to conserve oxygen and blood for the most important areas. Shock both protects and compounds the damage. The mind reacts differently, ignoring the pain and putting every effort into surviving. Fight-or-flight choices compete for dominance, and seconds become eons of confusion.

63

THE DUEL

*G*ino began his shift at 10:00 p.m. and set out in his cruiser, hoping for a peaceful night. However, early in the shift, he pulled over a speeding car and arrested the driver, who had a warrant for failing to appear in court. Gino took the driver to the barracks, where he would be held until his court appearance the next morning.

Around 2:00 a.m., Gino saw a U-Haul truck weaving in and out of the lanes on Route 95 in Warwick. Gino flipped on the lights and siren and pulled the car over. As he approached the passenger side of the vehicle, he motioned for the operator to roll down the window. He was slapped in the face by the smell of alcohol and marijuana. The female driver tried her level best to explain to Gino she only had a couple of drinks. Unfortunately, she was slurring her speech and couldn't tell him what time it was or count back from ten to one. Gino asked her to exit the vehicle. Despite her efforts, she fell off the car's side and landed on the ground. Gino checked her license and found out that her name was Stephanie, and she was from Coventry, Rhode Island.

Gino administered the field sobriety test to her, but after two tests, she fell to the ground, unable to complete them. Stephanie was arrested and taken back to the station. She made a phone call and told Gino she would take the breathalyzer test.

Her blood alcohol levels were 0.21 and 0.22, well above the .08 level, which indicates impairment. Following her arrest, Gino placed her in a cell at the Howard Barracks. As soon as Stephanie lay down on the thin mattress, she screamed out, "God, if you just take away this hangover and the humiliation of being arrested, I won't ever drink again."

A second cup of coffee gave him the boost he needed before he went back on the road. For the final hour of his shift, he returned to Route 95. He had been distracted from his fight with Renée and Michelle's visit to his mother by the activity of the last few hours.

On the highway, his mind raced. I know I want to get married sometime, but not right now. I need to focus on my career. Renée knows that, so why is she pushing the issue? Then I am avoiding another issue here, am I not? I thought Renée was the one, but is she? The debate continued in his head as he patrolled.

Gino's last traffic stop occurred on Route 95 at Route 37 in Warwick near Michelle's duplex. It was not uncommon for him to drive by Michelle's house every now and then. Curiosity and longing seemed to draw him.

When he drove by today, he hesitated because he usually drove by at night when she was sleeping. A new day had begun with the dawn. Hopefully a quick pass by the house would go unnoticed. He wanted to go by, but he was trying to avoid being seen. He drove by slowly and cautiously, his heart pounding in his chest, until he finally passed the house and continued down the street.

As Gino drove past the house, he never noticed the man lurking in the hedges across the street. Gino headed back toward the highway.

Suddenly, the tranquility of the early morning was shattered by gunshots. Gino felt a jolt of electricity shoot up his spine as he immediately realized that Michelle was in danger.

If he had been more observant, if he had spent more time driving around the neighborhood, this would not have happened. Michelle's house was just a block away, so there was no time for second-guessing.

He had to get there now!

64

THE RESCUE

She was thrown back by the force of the bullet. Michelle landed on the seat of her uniform pants after colliding with the garage door. Clutching her shoulder, she watched as the shooter escaped. Michelle was in shock. She couldn't comprehend what had just occurred, but she could feel the warm blood trickling from her wound.

When Gino asked, "Michelle, Michelle, where are you hit?" Michelle, in a fog, could only mutter, "I don't know."

Gino quickly examined her, noting a pained expression on her face and blood oozing from her shoulder. He then took her arm gently and said, "It looks like you took a pretty hard hit here."

Michelle nodded, still in shock, and Gino reassured her that she would be okay.

The fog cleared a bit. She shook her head and focused on his face. "Gino, what are you doing here?"

"Never mind that. How bad is it?" Gino asked.

As Michelle clutched her shoulder, she said, "I'm fine . . . or I will be. He was wearing dark clothes, a hooded sweatshirt, and a ski mask. He drove away in a green Ford Fairlane towards Warwick Ave. Now get the hell out of here and catch the bastard."

He screamed into his portable, "Twenty-eight to HQ, officer down! Officer down! Help needed at 30 Pensacola St., Warwick, Corporal Urban's house."

Gino tried to check her wound, but she pushed him away. "He can't get away!"

"Michelle, listen to me. You keep pressure on the wound and wait for the rescue. I'll get the son of a bitch," Gino's words were rushed, bordering on panic. "Motherfucker is a dead man."

Michelle started to argue, but the pain overwhelmed her. "Go, Gino, go."

Gino rushed to his cruiser. He screamed into his portable radio, "The suspect is traveling west on Post Road in a green Ford Fairlane, likely toward Route 95."

As troopers and officers called in, the radio erupted with calls offering assistance. The trooper on the desk calmly announced a rescue was on its way from the fire department.

Gino and others were immediately on the hunt. As he traveled down Route 1, he spotted a Ford Fairlane barreling down Post Road, and he called it in on the radio. The driver was weaving in and out of traffic. Two Warwick cruisers were coming up behind Gino.

"HQ to twenty-eight."

"Go ahead for twenty-eight."

"Do you have the vehicle in sight?"

"Yes, I do. He's driving north on Post Road. He just passed the airport and is heading toward Warwick-Cranston."

"Can you see the operator?"

"He has his hood up, but it's definitely a male."

"Thank you, twenty-eight. All units CODE RED. CODE RED!"

It was everyone's signal to stay off the air unless absolutely necessary. Gino and the two Warwick officers would be the focus of all attention. As Gino used all the power of the Plymouth Fury, he gained ground.

Gino focused on the Fairlane, which suddenly slowed down and drifted. After slowing and veering off the road, the vehicle crashed into a telephone pole in front of the Ice House on Post Road.

Gino and the Warwick officers approached with guns drawn. Gino shouted repeatedly at the driver. "Hands!" Gino shouted at him. "Turn your car off!"

The driver didn't answer, so Gino motioned to the Warwick officers to follow him up to the car. He approached the driver's side. A Warwick officer cleared the back seat while the other stood with a pump shotgun at the back of the Ford Fairlane.

As Gino approached, he could see a small revolver on the floor and the driver hunched over the steering wheel. Gino poked the driver with his free hand, and he didn't move. He reached in and pulled the driver off the steering wheel and back onto the seat. His sweatshirt was covered in blood, and it was pooling on the seat. Michelle's bullet had hit its mark. Gino felt for a pulse, but there was none.

Turning off the car, Gino said, "He's dead."

"Are you sure?" asked the Warwick Officer.

"Yeah, I'm sure, but keep that shotgun ready till I get that revolver out of the car."

"Will do."

Gino pulled the mask over the driver's head. Dead eyes stared into oblivion, and his face was frozen in death. It was Richard "Moon" Capelli's face. Gino was stunned and said, "I don't understand. What the fuck is he doing here? He was placed in witness protection seven years ago."

"You know this guy?" The Warwick officer asked.

"I knew him. I had him in protective custody for three years. We practically spent 24/7 together." Gino spoke, but inside, memories of his time with Moon were overloading his brain's capacity.

The other Warwick officer asked, "Why on Earth would he try to kill a trooper if he was in the program?"

"Not any trooper, but the trooper who helped him get out of jail for a crime he didn't commit," Gino answered.

"Well, she must have done something to piss off somebody."

The parking lot quickly filled up with cruisers. Captain Frank Muzerall arrived on the scene and took control. Evidence teams were called to Michelle's home and the crash scene. The medical examiner had been called, and both locations were surrounded by yellow police tape.

Gino filled the captain in on the events leading up to the crash.

"Captain, how's Michelle? Just a flesh wound, right?"

"She's at RI Hospital in stable condition, but in surgery. That's all I know."

"Permission to go to the hospital, Captain?"

"Go ahead, but detectives will want a statement from you, so stay on your portable."

"Will do, Cap."

65

THE THIN BLUE LINE

Corporal Michelle Urban's friends and troopers jammed the lobby at RI Hospital. Small clusters of men and women talked to Colonel Culhaney and the attorney general.

Faces of concern and whispers greeted Gino as he glided through the revolving door.

Gino saluted the colonel.

"Colonel, how is she?"

"She's in the ICU. Her dad's with her."

"ICU, sir? I thought the bullet just grazed her."

"They took her to surgery to clean out her wound, and her blood pressure dropped."

"Thank you very much, sir. I would like to wait with everyone if you don't mind," Gino said.

"Peterson, you did a nice job today. Lucky break that you were close to the crime scene. I wanted you to know the detectives found a file on your late father's accident at the scene. It appears that the corporal had launched her own investigation."

Gino wondered why she was investigating his dad's death and if it had anything to do with Moon shooting her.

The colonel said to Gino: "Feel free to stay as long as you like. It's no secret that you two have a history together."

After Colonel Walter Smith retired three years ago, Colonel Culhaney became superintendent. Gino wasn't surprised to learn that he knew. There would be talk about what happened in the Intelligence Unit for years.

Gino walked over to a group of academy classmates who gathered in one corner. A doctor entered from the operating room through the double doors. Her lab coat was close enough for Gino to see the words stitched on it—Chief of Surgery, Dr. Kara Leonard.

She introduced herself, then pointed to the men in white coats standing on either side of her. Leonard pointed to her left and then to her right, "This is Dr. Elliot Richardson and Dr. Raul de la Porta. Michelle is under our care."

Taking a moment to glance down at a file folder, Leonard said, "On behalf of Michelle's father, I'd like to thank all of you for attending." Leonard looked into eyes of concern.

"In the course of the surgery to clean out her wound, Michelle went into shock. Mr. Urban has given me permission to share this with you. Our ICU is treating her with IV fluids and antibiotics. She is sedated and not in pain. It's just a matter of waiting and hoping she comes out of it, but only time will tell."

When Leonard finished, the colonel said, "Thank you, Doctor. On behalf of the state police, I thank you for the care you are providing to Michelle."

Nodding, the doctors turned around and disappeared behind the swinging doors. In his anxiety, Gino viewed them as aliens, scurrying back to the mothership after speaking with Earth's inhabitants.

Culhaney turned to the crowd that by now had nearly doubled in size. "I have two major concerns. The first is obviously the corporal's recovery. The second is the unsuccessful attempt on her life. It's quite possible this is not just the act of one man, and if so, we have to assume they will try again."

The Colonel explained to them that they would be setting up a detail to keep Michelle safe. "Captain Muzerall will be giving out assignments. Detectives will continue investigating the shooting. Everyone else should go back to work or go home and rest."

Gino assumed that since he was working overnight, he would be sent home. Gino saw Captain Muzerall talking to two detectives. He wanted to volunteer to work security.

"Peterson, stay here. You're on the security detail. Report to the ICU break room. They're setting up there."

"Captain, I worked all night, and—"

Muzerall interrupted him, "Peterson, Michelle's father, Lt. Urban, asked you to stay. So you're staying."

"Yes, sir, Captain."

66

RENÉE FACES REALITY

Gino called his mom and Renée to let them know what had happened and that he was now assigned to a security detail. Teresa expressed relief that Michelle was safe and promised to pray for her. The call to Renée did not go as well.

"Gino, are you all right? You worried me so much. Are you coming home soon?"

"I have been assigned to Michelle's security detail," Gino said.

An icy silence followed.

"I hope she recovers fully, but why are you there?" Renée asked. "I don't want you to be there. Aren't your professional and private relationships screaming for you not to be there?"

Gino could hear Renée sniffling. "Renée, please listen to me," he said gently. "Her father asked me to be involved in the security detail. You know he's a retired trooper, and I can't say no."

"Okay, let me get this straight. Her father asks you to stay and you do. I ask you to come home and you can't?"

Gino replied, "Renée, it's my job. They assigned me the detail."

He realized that halfway through his sentence the line was dead.

67

ADDICTION

Captain Muzerall scheduled Michelle's detail to work twelve-hour shifts. The ICU break room was equipped with monitors connected to hospital security cameras.

Hospital security was responsible for all floors except the ICU. Three troopers were assigned three posts: one trooper worked on the monitors, one outside Michelle's room, and one at the ICU doors. Troopers rotated between the three posts each shift. The first night passed quietly, and after getting off at 8:00 a.m., Gino chose to sleep at the Howard Barracks rather than at home.

Michelle's shooting, Moon's unexpected return and death, and his issues with Renée all became convenient excuses to take more pills. And so the love affair between Gino and Vicodin continued. All the pills from this prescription were consumed in half the time. In need of more, he contacted his physician.

"My name is Gino Peterson, and I am calling to refill my Vicodin prescription." A harried receptionist asked for his date of birth. Gino wasn't scheduled for a refill for another two weeks, she explained.

It was as if Gino was struck by a tsunami of anxiety. His skin was cold and clammy. Most of all, he feared losing the fuel he relied on to shield him from reality.

Gino decided to take the direct approach. "May I speak to Doctor Birnbaum, please?"

"Mr. Peterson, I'll give your number to the doctor."

"Okay, thank you," Gino said.

His anxiety made him want to demand to speak to the doctor, but he resisted. Despite his desperation, he didn't want to draw that much attention to himself.

Gino was scheduled to start work at 8:00 p.m., so he hoped the doctor would contact him by then.

Dr. Ariel Birnbaum, Gino's highly regarded orthopedic surgeon whose father was a Long Island police chief, had a soft spot for cops but was not easily fooled. He called Gino after his last patient of the day.

"Hello," Gino said.

As always, Dr. Birnbaum's voice was calm. "Mr. Peterson, Dr. Birnbaum here. I understand you want more Vicodin, but you should have two weeks of the medication on hand."

"My back is killing me, and I forgot to tell your receptionist that I lost my prescription bottle while moving. It happened yesterday while moving from my apartment to my new one."

In a stern voice, "Gino, I've been telling you for months that physical therapy and pain medication were only temporary solutions. If you want to eliminate your bulging disc pain, you need surgery."

"Dr. B, if you could just give me two weeks of pills to replace the ones I lost, I will schedule the surgery. I promise." Gino was begging.

Dr. Birnbaum had other calls to make an hour before his surgery. "I'm going to accept your explanation about losing your prescription, but you must come to my office at nine o'clock on Monday morning. You will receive two weeks' worth of Vicodin from me, but you should know that this is the last prescription I will write for that medication. They are controlled substances for a reason, and you can become addicted to them."

"It's nothing like that, Dr. B. Thank you, and I'll see you on Monday."

"Goodbye, Mr. Peterson," Dr. B. ended the call.

Gino arrived at work at 8:00 p.m. and stood outside Michelle's door. Michelle was comfortably resting, and the ventilator was breathing rhythmically.

In the early hours of the morning, nurse Donna McKenna pushed the med cart down the corridor. Gino had met her when the detail began.

She was about twenty-five years old and just beginning her career. She wore blue scrubs and a vest adorned with a stethoscope and employee identification. If Gino had something other than getting high on his mind, he would have noticed her bright blue eyes that weren't dulled by the blue scrubs and the brown hair surrounding a perfectly proportioned face. Beneath the scrubs lay an ample figure. In addition to the hospital ID, the key for the med cart was on a lanyard around her neck.

Donna sang Beatles songs as she moved the cart from room to room. The cart stopped opposite Michelle's room, and she greeted Gino.

Donna unlocked the med cart and poured two pills into a white pill cup.

A buzzer and bell sounded when Donna entered the patient's room. "Code blue, code blue, ICU room 42 A," the intercom screamed.

Gino watched as nurse McKenna rushed past him toward the other end of the ICU. He looked up and down the corridor and didn't see anyone. Most of the staff were in room 42 A, attending to the patient.

Gino peeked into the room. The pills were still on the bedside table next to the patient. He entered because he dreaded the upcoming weekend without pain medication.

The whiteboard on the wall caught his attention. It listed nurse Donna McKenna and patient Lisa Chin.

Lisa was snoring loudly. The paper cup was still there, and Gino looked at two blue pills. They looked like Vicodin, but because of their different colors, he wasn't sure.

His first thought was that they must be painkillers. He was so desperate that he was willing to take the risk of taking pills when he did not know what they were. As he stared at them, they grew larger and larger and called to him.

To hell with that, he thought. He reached for the pills.

Nurse McKenna startled him, "Trooper, can I help you?"

"No, no, sorry, I thought she was in distress, but I guess she was just snoring."

She hesitated for a moment and pushed the thought that he might be after pain medication from her mind. He was, after all, a state trooper.

"She's fine, Trooper. I'll take it from here."

68

MICHELLE AWAKENS

A week after the shooting, Michelle was still on a ventilator. Gino felt the need to be there, and not just as part of the security detail. Investigating his father's death had put her in danger. He desperately wanted to be there when she came back to herself.

Wearing casual clothes from his locker, Gino slept in the Lincoln Barracks. Most of his meals were obtained from hospital vending machines. He took more of the pills Dr. B gave him to numb the pain. When he fell at the barracks after returning from the hospital, whispers began. He just mumbled when asked if he was all right.

He called Renée every day, but she never answered. Gino left several messages without success. Ultimately, he chose to leave her alone, let her cool off, and then speak with her.

Gino spoke with the detectives who confirmed that Michelle's Beretta fired the bullet that killed Capelli.

According to his handler at the US Marshals Service, he had been AWOL for three months. When they asked his nephew, Aldo, why his uncle had returned, he said he didn't know anything and hadn't seen his uncle in years.

Considering Moon's past, they tried to connect him to the mob, but that was a dead end. They even used Michelle's file and tried to connect Moon to Gino's father's death but ran into more dead ends.

The investigation would continue. Moon's return to avenge his two mafia buddies' deaths seemed like the only plausible explanation.

At the barracks, Gino was asleep when a trooper hollered up, "Peterson, Peterson."

"Yeah, yeah, I'm up."

"You have been asked to come to the hospital by Corporal Urban's father."

"What did he say? Is she okay?" Gino sounded a bit desperate.

"It was just that he asked for you. Get your ass down there, and you can ask him yourself."

Gino always seemed to be in a fog or distracted and his fellow troopers were becoming impatient and didn't trust him. Gino's recent perpetual mind fog posed a potential threat to the lives of his fellow troopers. If he were impaired and required to assist a colleague, there was no assurance that he could effectively carry out his duties. Despite this, Gino swiftly got dressed, grabbed the keys to a cruiser, and rushed to the hospital.

When he arrived at the ICU, he found troopers packing up their equipment.

As Gino walked down the corridor, he noticed Mr. Urban standing outside Michelle's door.

"Is something wrong? Is she okay?" Ted Urban grabbed Gino's shoulders as he sensed his frantic concern. Then he turned Gino toward Michelle's bed. As she sat in bed, she smiled. The IV and ventilator had been removed. There was a look of weakness and fatigue on her face.

"Gino, she wants to talk to you." Gino walked into the room and sat in the chair next to her bed.

"Hi, Gino," Michelle said softly.

"Michelle. Hi. How are you feeling?"

"Like I've been shot." She laughed a bit.

"You had everyone worried."

"Sorry."

"No need to feel sorry," Gino said.

Michelle's voice was hoarse from the ventilator tube.

"When the detectives told me Moon shot me, I couldn't believe he was back. What could I have done to him? I've gone over it in my mind a thousand times and nothing."

It was Gino's choice not to let her know about the most recent theory since theories, in law enforcement, are only theories until evidence is found. Facts are the enemy of theories.

"The detectives hit a dead end as to motive and couldn't find a connection to the Raimondi family," Gino explained.

Michelle took a breath and winced as Gino continued, "They even tried to connect him to my father's death, nothing."

Gino asked why the security detail was ending.

"I'm being discharged today, and they're going to set up security at my house. I'm going to be staying there while I recover."

Gino could tell Michelle was tired. "Michelle, you need to rest." She reached out for Gino's hand as he left.

As he took it, he felt a sense of vulnerability and softness. "Thank you, Gino, for saving my life. I might have died if you hadn't come by."

As Gino squeezed her hand, he looked down at the floor and murmured, "Just doing my job, just like you. It will be easy to talk more about what happened when you get home."

69

"DEAR JOHN"

Gino decided it was time to talk to Renée at home. He didn't know whether either of them had the emotional energy to mend the relationship.

After turning the key, he entered the apartment. "Renée, it's me." There was no response, only the echo of his voice. When Gino walked into their bedroom, he found her closet and bureau empty. Her personal items were all taken. As police jargon has it, she fled the scene.

His bathroom cabinet contained the last of his Vicodin. This was definitely a Vicodin-filled day for him. A large white pill, oval-shaped and creased in the middle, had enslaved him.

It was beyond comprehension how something so small could overcome a person's will. Opioids chemically repurposed the brain in an unstoppable manner. Renée tried to stop him, but he ignored her.

He noticed a small envelope on the kitchen table. After downing the Vicodin, Gino sat down to read it.

Dear Gino,

I am sorry to have to write this. It would have been better if I had done it in person. I haven't returned your calls because I was hoping you would just come home. It is clear to me now that even if you did come home, you would be somewhere else in your mind. Although I thought being with you was the right thing for me, it wasn't. There would always be someone between us. Gino, you're a good man, but you've made your choice, and now you must follow your heart. I am determined to follow my heart and hope to find someone who is truly committed to me.

My best wishes are with you,

Renée

P.S. Please get off the pills; they're going to ruin you!

As Gino got up from the kitchen table, he flopped down on the couch. His ruined relationships occupied his thoughts. Had he brought baggage from Michelle's relationship to Renée? Was Renée happy living with him? Michelle was on his mind a lot, obviously too much. I lost both of them. Renée wrote, "Follow your heart," but he didn't know where his heart was leading him.

70

VERMONT
Two Years Ago

Eight people sat in a semicircle on folding chairs in the basement of St. Anthony's Church in Colchester, Vermont. Behind them, a small stage was decorated for the Christmas pageant. Dark mahogany paneling covered the walls. They were adorned with images of saints who stared down at you with judgment in their eyes. The scent of burned coffee and stale pastries filled the air. The group met every Wednesday at 7:00 p.m. They gathered to soothe their souls.

"Hi, my name is Gino, and I'm addicted to pain meds."

"Hey, Gino," came the reply.

"The last time I took a pill was eight weeks ago. I didn't intend to become an addict, but here I am. My journey began when I hurt my back, was prescribed pain medication, and lost my way. There was a promise that the pills would ease the pain. The physical pain was taken away, but never the pain I felt inside. Instead, they almost destroyed my life.

"During my time here, I've learned that I was just trying to bury the pain I had inside of me. When I was fifteen, I lost my dad. They called it an accident, but I never believed it. My guess is that someone drove him off the road, but I never really had the courage to investigate. My only desire was to bury the hurt and loss I felt.

"At first, I tried to bury it by joining the state police and using my macho facade to wall off everyone in my life to my pain.

"When that didn't work, I tried to drown my brain with more and more pills. Only in the last eight weeks have I learned that to move on, I have to process his loss.

"Now I have the skills to deal with my pain, to begin healing, and to move on with my life without the crutch of narcotics.

"Thank you."

As tears welled up in his eyes, they stood and applauded. Rather than brushing them aside, he let them flow. He then embraced everyone in the circle.

It was hard to believe eight weeks had gone by since Gino told his supervisor he was checking himself into the inpatient program. His last night at the hospital guarding Michelle was, in many ways, his low point. Due to his addiction, he had considered stealing pain medication from patients. He was so close to being arrested for stealing drugs or ending the nurse's career by blaming her.

Today, he would go home and face his demons outside of the controlled environment of the recovery center. The counseling sessions would continue, and he would take it one day at a time. Gino said goodbye to his counselors and fellow patients. One of his counselors dropped him off at the Amtrak station at White River Junction, and he boarded the train to Providence.

As he passed through the Green Mountains of Vermont to the plains of Rhode Island, he thought of all the things he had been through and prayed for wisdom to not make the same mistakes. They say you learn from your mistakes, and Gino thought if that was true, he would end up a very wise man because he made plenty of them.

He thought about the stigma he would face from his fellow troopers for seeking help for an addiction. He dreaded the idea of his colleagues looking down on him for getting help. They would say that as cops, we have to suck it up and overcome the stressors of our lives and profession. We cannot take drugs to fight off reality. He knew that many people in law enforcement saw addiction as a sign of weakness. If you were addicted to drugs, you should just stop; use your willpower. He feared that his peers would judge him and think he was not fit to serve as a police officer.

Perhaps someday, they would understand addiction.

Teresa was the only person he talked to while he was in the program and was, as expected, very supportive. She was proud of the strength he displayed in asking for help. They talked about family and the old neighborhood. They never spoke about Michelle or Renée.

71

MOON DELIVERS GINO A MESSAGE

Gino arrived home around 10:00 p.m., and as he entered the apartment, he could tell that Teresa had kept it clean and collected his mail, as she insisted she would. The mail was arranged neatly. Piles of envelopes and fliers were on the kitchen table, and one package awaited his attention.

Although Teresa had stocked the refrigerator with all his favorites, including lasagna, he wasn't hungry. He decided on seltzer water, sat down at his kitchen table, and sorted through the mail.

Gino opened the package last. When he opened it, a set of keys, a cassette tape, and a note fell onto the table. "To Gino" was written on an envelope. He tore it open and read:

If you're reading this, I must be dead. First of all, Aldo is a smart kid, but he is in over his head with this crew. I would appreciate it if you kept an eye on him. The keys are for the car Lou Raimondi used to force your dad off the road. Another key is for a garage where the car is stored. The address is on the key's tab. You will find a bloody shirt in the trunk. In a fistfight, your dad kicked Lou Raimondi's ass. Because Louie couldn't handle losing, he followed your father and ran him off the road. I'm sure you're wondering how I know all this. Lou came to me in a panic after the accident and told me that he was in a jam. Since your dad was a civilian, he didn't want his old man to know what he did. As for the bloody shirt and the car, he told me to get rid of them.

Gino, you know me well. When I deal with someone, I always get an insurance policy. Louie was never someone I could trust. I kept the car instead of dumping it. I switched the cassette player I had in my pocket to record as soon as I returned to the club, he asked me if everything was okay. Then he told me everything that happened that night. That your dad was pissed that he was still after your mom. That night they got into a fight just outside Pete's Spa. After following your dad, he ran him off the road. If

*that's not enough to convict the SOB, you're not the
cop I thought you were.*

I'll be waiting for you on the other side.

Moon

Gino's first call was to the supervisor of the crime scene unit at headquarters. Gino informed Lt. Cindy Ballou about the package he received.

In thirty minutes, she would alert the rest of her unit, and they would arrive to collect the evidence. They would complete their work by morning, and based on what Gino told Ballou, there would be sufficient evidence for an arrest warrant.

Gino called Michelle after Lt. Ballou left his apartment. Her husky voice groaned as she answered, "Hello."

Gino said, "I'm sorry to wake you up, but I have something to tell you." Gino then told her about the contents of the package he received from Moon.

Next, he asked, "Michelle, are you interested in ruining somebody's morning stroll around Lincoln Woods?"

Michelle brushed away the remaining cobwebs, "Yes, I would very much like that."

▪ The End ▪

ACKNOWLEDGMENTS

Like many other books, this was a collaborative endeavor. The most crucial collaborator was Stuart Horwitz of Book Architecture, who served as the architect of this story while I played the role of the laborer. Susan Pohlman, my copyeditor, lent her keen eyes and story sense to keep the narrative on track.

Jen Neves Bissonnette, responsible for the author's photo, is a true friend with incredible talent. Her artistic vision brings the author's image to life. For a cover I could never have imagined, I thank Molly Regan of Logica Design. Thank you also to the good folks of 1106 Design for the interior design, proofreading, and innumerable other small but crucial tasks.

I thank Vince Petronio for his lifelong friendship and assistance with the story. His insights and support significantly shaped the narrative. I'm also thankful to Lisa, my administrative assistant, who was instrumental in preparing the manuscript.

I express my heartfelt appreciation and love to my family, who are the reason why every day is worth living. Their unwavering support and love have been the bedrock of my journey.